A PRIVATE WALTZ

Without a word Hugh traversed the distance between him and Sara. With every step he took, Sara's heart beat a little faster. When he was at last standing before her, standing so close she could reach out and touch him, he, instead, touched her. One of his strong hands snaked about her waist and the other clasped her hand in a light but compelling grip. Still silent, his grey eyes locked in a gaze with her blue ones, he took a step. Sara followed. Before she could even realize what they were about she found that she was dancing with Hugh Deverill down the length of the gallery.

She never tried to resist. Indeed, Sara found she could only stare up at him, conscious only of his arm about her waist, of her own small hand enveloped in the warmth of his own. At school Sara had taken lessons in dance, but no amount of tutelage could have prepared her for the sensation of being held in a man's arms. She felt as if she had suffered a small electric shock and her breath came to her in small little wisps.

Again and again they circled the room, and Hugh's arm tightened about her, drawing her closer to him, his gaze never wavering from her face . . .

Books by Nancy Lawrence

DELIGHTFUL DECEPTION

A SCANDALOUS SEASON

ONCE UPON A CHRISTMAS

A NOBLE ROGUE

Published by Zebra Books

A NOBLE ROGUE

Nancy Lawrence

Zebra Books
Kensington Publishing Corp.

http://www.zebrabooks.com

ZEBRA BOOKS are published by

Kensington Publishing Corp.
850 Third Avenue
New York, NY 10022

Zebra and the Z logo Reg. U.S. Pat. & TM Off.

First Printing: September, 1998
10 9 8 7 6 5 4 3 2 1

Printed in the United States of America

Chapter One

Miss Sara Brandon-Howe surveyed the kitchens in stunned silence. Her expression, usually quite animated, was frozen into a curious mask of bewilderment and horror.

For a moment she could do nothing more than stand in the doorway. She held her bandbox in one hand while her other hand clutched at the neck of her pelisse in a vain attempt to combat the chill of a June breeze that blew against her back through the open entry.

The kitchen was in disarray. Everywhere she turned, Sara saw dirt, discarded food, and broken dishes. Even more confounding were the sounds that emanated from the various corners and coves of the room.

She clearly heard a woman softly sobbing. From the direction of the buttery she heard a man's voice indulging in a hearty string of alarming French oaths. Punctuating all was the distinctive sound of crashing crockery.

Sara slammed the kitchen door shut and demanded, in

a voice loud enough to be heard over the din of smashing pottery, "What in heaven's name is occurring?"

The kitchen fell to silence and a small man of dark looks emerged from the buttery. His angry countenance was not the least familiar to her.

"Who are you?" she asked in a voice of authority. "And who gave you leave to destroy these kitchens in such a fashion?"

"The little king gave me leave when he refused my wages," replied the man with an impudent accent. He added a codicil in French that included some rather round terms Sara had never had occasion to learn during the course of her extensive lessons at Miss Pembleton's School for Gentlewomen.

The words she was able to interpret made little sense to her. "I don't understand. What little king?"

"He means Master Philip—I mean, Lord Carville," said a young woman as she emerged from her hiding place behind an oak cupboard. Her eyes were puffy from crying and the course of her tears had left telltale streaks down her pale cheeks. Sara immediately recognized her as one of the housemaids who had served at Carvington Hall for years.

"Daisy, is that you? Daisy, come out from there and explain what this horrid man is talking about."

Daisy used her apron to wipe at her eyes, then used it again to jab at the still angry Frenchman. "That's Monsieur Henri, the cook," she said.

Henri's face turned an alarming shade of red. "I am a chef, not a cook!" he sputtered. "You *Anglais!* You know nothing! I have prepared meals for the royalty of Europe! How *dare* you call me a cook!"

"Yes, of course! And you're a very excellent chef, I am certain," said Sara, thinking it best, for the moment at least, to appease the volatile man. "But you must not interrupt while Daisy explains what has occurred to so upset you."

Daisy complied by issuing a fresh tide of tears. "Oh, miss! We had no idea you was to come home now after all this time! And to such a welcome!"

"Daisy, you musn't cry. Only tell me what could have possessed this man to have done all this!" Sara gestured with one gloved hand at the mayhem that once constituted a kitchen.

"It's like Monsieur Henri said, miss. Master Philip—I mean, Lord Carville—he won't pay us. Monsieur Henri and me, we're the only ones left. All the other servants have gone off long ago."

Sara could hardly credit Daisy's words. "Do you mean there are no servants left? On the entire estate? Daisy, you must be mistaken! My brother would never turn off all the servants!"

"Oh, no, miss! The servants weren't sacked. They left once Lord Carville stopped paying wages. Mrs. Basham was the last to go. She tried to stay on, bless her. Said she could no more leave this house than cut off her own hand. But in the end, she left, too."

Sara was quite stunned by this news. "But Mrs. Basham has been the housekeeper here at Carvington Hall since Philip and I were children. She was trusted and loved and—why, she was more a member of the family than she was a servant!"

"And so says she the day she packed her bags and left," said Daisy, sadly. "Off to her sister she went, leaving only me here."

Feeling a trifle overwhelmed by Daisy's words, Sara untied the neat ribboned bow from beneath her chin and removed the demure straw bonnet that covered her light brown curls. She set her bonnet and bandbox down on the only clean place left on the table. "It was good of you to stay on, Daisy."

"Well, I don't have a sister to go to," said the maid, reasonably.

"I see. As bad as that, is it?"

"Well, I could do without wages, I supposed. Lord Carville has always been kind to me and as long as I had a room of me own and somethin' to eat, it weren't too bad, I supposed. That is, until he came home from London yesterday with Monsieur Henri here." Daisy jerked her head in the Frenchman's direction. "Lord Carville wanted Monsieur Henri to cook for his guests—two gentlemen who came down from London—so Monsieur Henri took me with him to the shops today to buy what he needed. But the shops wouldn't sell to him unless he paid something toward Carvington Hall's accounts. So Monsieur Henri, he comes back, fit for fury. He went to Lord Carville in the library—bold as you please!—and demanded to know if Lord Carville was done up."

"*Il est pouvré!*" declared Henri in disgust.

Sara cast him a sharp look. "My brother is *not* poor!"

"But, miss, I'm afraid he is," said Daisy, laying a gentle hand upon her sleeve. "I told Lord Carville then about the shops, you see. I asked him to give me just a bit to pay against the accounts, so the shopkeepers would be satisfied and would sell to Monsieur chef here. But Lord Carville said there was no money to be had. So then Monsieur Henri, he demanded to know if there was any money to pay his wages! When Lord Carville said he'd have to wait and see, Monsieur Henri said he was going back to London, first thing. He said some other things, too, but they were in French, so I can't imagine what they meant."

Sara, however, could very well imagine what the Frenchman had said. She turned to him with a look of censure. "I think both of you have come by the wrong conclusion!

My brother, Philip, is far from impoverished! In fact, my brother and I enjoy a most comfortable income so you need have no fear about receiving your just compensation."

Daisy looked doubtful. "Yes, miss, but—"

"I really don't know how you got your facts so muddled, Daisy. Surely you know neither Philip nor I would ever be found in such financial straits as you describe!"

Daisy frowned. "Oh, but, miss! Lord Carville said—"

"I am sure my brother said a great many things, all of which you appear to have misunderstood. Now, Daisy, I shall speak with my brother and try to determine just how his innocent words might have been taken so amiss. We shall clear all up presently. But you, sir," she continued, turning her attention upon the Frenchman, "you present another matter. I am afraid I cannot forgive the damage you have done here nor can I countenance employing such a horridly vengeful man as you appear to be! I should think it best for all concerned if you carried forward your plan to leave Carvington Hall immediately."

She drew her reticule from her arm and began to search its contents. "Hard as I find it to believe such a thing, I must take you at your word when you say you are owed wages. What sum?"

The Frenchman fixed her with a potent stare and named a figure that brought Sara's head up with a snap.

"I don't believe it!" she said, astonished. "Philip promised you that much money just to prepare his meals? Why, it's positively sinful! I—I won't pay it!"

The healthy string of epithets the Frenchman rattled off went a long way toward changing her mind. She didn't understand half the things he said in his native tongue, but she was well able to read the expression on his face. A desperate wish to preserve the last of the remaining crockery caused her to dip her hand into her reticule and withdraw a number of notes.

"Here! Take this!" she said, thrusting the money into his hands. "It is all I can spare. Now, do go, please!"

He obeyed without further protest and Sara breathed a decided sigh of relief at his departure.

"What a horrid little man! Whatever could have possessed Philip to have hired him? I hate to think what he shall say once he sees the state of these kitchens!" she added, taking a more thorough look about her than she had before.

"Oh, miss, I shall make it all tidy again," said Daisy, quickly. "It's not so very much, after all. I'm certain I can have the kitchens back to rights before Lord Carville returns."

"Returns? Do you mean my brother is not at home?" asked Sara.

"Oh, he's out with the two London gentlemen," Daisy said. "Left this afternoon, they did, looking quite smart, especially Lord Carville. He cuts *such* a dash. I heard him tell Henri to expect them back for dinner."

"I see," said Sara, with a small frown. "No wonder he wasn't there to meet me at the coaching inn. I waited and waited and when he didn't come I had to abandon my trunks at the inn and make my way home on my own. Daisy, is it possible Philip could have forgotten about my coming home today?"

She had her answer in Daisy's rather pained expression. "Well, you know, Master Philip has had much on his plate ever since he succeeded your father."

"But Daisy, my papa passed away well over a year ago. Besides, I have been away at school almost these two years past. Didn't—didn't he miss me?"

Daisy regarded her in some alarm, on the watch for any signs of impending tears. But Miss Sara Brandon-Howe was neither so young nor so prone to emotion as her nineteen years might have led one to believe. In the two years she had spent at Miss Pembleton's School for Gentlewomen, she had learned her lessons well. While she could admit in her heart that her homecoming was far from that which she had imagined it would be, she would never dream of admitting such a thing to a housemaid.

Still, she was deeply disappointed to find Philip not about. She was anxious to see him, for theirs had always been a close relationship. Philip was her senior by five years and he had always proved to be an indulgent older brother. Even as children, he had been unaffected by jealousies and quite willing to allow her to follow at his heels whenever he went off fishing or hunting or learning to jump the low fences in the fields. He had been comforting and caring when their mother had died, and when their father had passed away, they had cried together and consoled each other, strengthening the secure bond that already existed between them.

Hurtful indeed was it for Sara to realize that Philip was not on hand to greet her after she had been away from home at school for so long.

As if reading her mistress's thoughts, Daisy said, "I shouldn't jump to judgment too quick, miss. After all, those two gentlemen from London take up quite a bit of Lord Carville's time since they arrived."

"I see," said Sara again, although she was not at all sure she did see. After a moment she straightened her shoulders slightly, and said, "Well, they shan't have that advantage now that I am here, for I intend to see that Philip spends time with *me*. I have been gone too long at school and I have missed Philip and my home and everything about this beloved place. And now that I have learned everything an accomplished young lady should know about running a household and serving as mistress of a manor, I intend to turn my newfound knowledge toward setting this house to rights!"

Daisy brightened. "I should like that very much, miss. So should Master Philip, too, if he would but consider it."

"Then we shall begin now. Daisy, if you will set to work putting the kitchens in order, I shall begin preparing our dinner."

"*You,* miss?" uttered Daisy, horrified by the very idea.

"There is no one else to do it, I think, now that Henri is turned off. I can only hope Philip and his guests don't expect from me a dinner such as they were served last night by the hand of a French chef!"

"Oh, Henri didn't cook last night," said Daisy. "He took one look at the meager cupboards in this kitchen and refused to lift a finger. I thought Lord Carville was going to pop, that's how angry he was and he scolded Monsieur Henri forever, that's how it did seem. But he might as well have spoken to the cat for all the good it did, for still Monsieur Henri refused to cook."

"Then who prepared their dinner last night?"

"I did," said Daisy, making a face. "And none of the gentlemen touched a bite!"

"Well, we cannot have Philip and his friends starving to death. Never fear! I may not be a master of the kitchen on the order of a French chef, but I've learned a thing or two at school and I promise I shan't set a shabby table for Philip and his guests!" Sara drew off her gloves and pelisse, saying, "When Philip returns, we shall deal with fetching my trunks from the coaching inn and then I may take the time to settle myself and unpack. In the meantime, let us have a look at the larder, shall we?"

She set to work immediately, first taking inventory of the contents of the larder and the buttery, and planning her menu from their limited supplies. Some time later she was able to assure herself that she had created a most respectable meal in two courses and four removes. She dispatched Daisy to lay the covers in the dining room and was setting the final garnish on a small basket of fruits when she heard the muted chorus of distinctly male voices coming from the direction of the hall.

Sara took the time to remove her apron and wipe her hands before she hurried to the hall. Philip was there alone, standing in the shadows, discarding his gloves and hat on a nearby table. "Philip!" she cried in a tremulously happy voice.

He turned then and saw her, and came forward a little into the center of the hall where the light shone more brightly upon his face.

Sara shared many of her brother's characteristics: they each had large, expressive blue eyes, straight noses, and delicately lined lips. They were both slim and of slight build; in Philip, this trait was manifested by a lanky, rather loose-limbed manner of walking; in Sara, it defined her movements as uncommonly graceful.

But on this evening, it would have been difficult to detect any similarities between them. Many months had passed since last Sara had seen her brother and she was rather shocked to find that he was not looking well. The color had left his complexion and his blue eyes were surrounded by shadows. He was dressed in the height of fashion and at the age of six-and-twenty cut a very dashing figure. However, she thought, no amount of tailoring or wadding in the elegantly fashioned coat he wore could disguise the fact that he was much thinner than she remembered.

"Sara?" he murmured, unsure. "By Jove, it *is* you!" He smiled then, which she read as an invitation to throw herself into his brotherly arms.

"Oh, Philip! How I've missed you!"

"By all that's holy! You gave me quite a start just now!" he said, taking her by the shoulders and setting her back a step. "There now! Mind my new waistcoat, if you please, Miss Sassy! When did you arrive?"

"Hours ago!" she said, warmed to hear him use the name he had called her as a child. "And I've been waiting for you! Philip, didn't you get my letter? I wrote to you, saying I'd be home from school this day. How could you forget?"

He had the good grace to look slightly abashed. "Was it *today?*" he asked, rather weakly. "The devil of it is, I forgot all about it. Not about your homecoming, for I couldn't forget that!" he said quickly, giving her cheek a gentle cuff to stem the protest he saw forming on her lips. "I merely forgot which day, is all. Now don't fly up, Sara, for you know I would have met you if only I'd remembered! But the thing is, I've been so curst busy these last months, what with running Carvington Hall and traveling to the London house pretty frequently, I can tell you!"

Sara scanned his pale, drawn face with sympathetic eyes. "You have quite a few cares and worries, don't you?"

"I never thought about it before, but I guess I do," said Philip, after a moment's consideration.

"But now that I'm here, I can be of tremendous help to you," Sara said. "I shall especially help with setting the Hall to rights. Philip, you'll never *believe* when I tell you what Daisy said!"

"Daisy? The maid?" he asked, suddenly watchful.

Sara nodded. "Daisy said all the servants had gone off because they weren't being paid! And that horrid French chef said—" She broke off at the unexpected sound of male laughter coming from the direction of the first floor drawing room.

Philip heard the voices, too, and was clearly distracted by them. "French chef? Oh! You mean Henri!"

"Yes, and I'm afraid I have something to confess to you,

Philip. You see, I came upon him in the kitchens, and he was creating the most horrid row—"

"I wouldn't pay him any mind. He's French, after all, and likes to rattle on about creating art with food or some such nonsense!"

Another wave of deep, masculine laughter issued from the direction of the drawing room and Philip unconsciously began to move toward it, as if responding to a siren's song.

Sara clasped his hand to draw his attention. "But that's what I'm trying to tell you. You see, Daisy was crying and the pottery was breaking and—Oh, I'm explaining this very badly!"

Philip frowned and disentangled his hand from hers. "Here, now, Sara! We'll speak of this later!"

"But, Philip, where are you going? Aren't you glad to see me returned home?"

"The thing is, I've got guests! Can't keep them waiting! We'll speak later!" He glanced anxiously up in the direction of the drawing room and crossed the hall toward the stair.

"But, Philip, I have so much to tell you!" she said, in a rather bewildered voice, and she took an uncertain step or two after him.

"Not now, dash it!" he said gruffly, and he began his ascent up the great staircase. "Tell Henri we shall be ready to dine in half an hour. Daisy may wait on table. There's a good girl!" He looked back at her as he reached the landing. There was no mistaking the look of confused injury on his sister's face, and his expression softened slightly. "Sara, I *am* glad to have you home, but the deuce of it is that I have guests and—well, I must not keep them waiting. *You* understand! There's a girl! Now, be a good sister and tell Henri he may serve dinner in a half-hour."

For a moment Sara was too stunned to speak. But by

the time she had gathered her wits about her and had the good sense to yet again attempt to tell her brother that Henri had been turned off, Philip had already disappeared up the stairs and into the drawing room, closing the door behind him.

Chapter Two

Staring out the window of the best guest bedchamber at Carvington Hall, Mr. Hugh Deverill watched the lengthening shadows of evening stretch across the parklands of the estate. For a moment he imagined himself out there in the last remaining light of the summer day, seated in his curricle with Lambert beside him, driving away from Carvington Hall as fast as his highly bred horses could take him.

His valet, unaware of his master's musings, attempted to draw his attention to the task of selecting a coat for dinner. Hugh waved him away, saying, idly, "You decide, Lambert. To own the truth, I don't much care what I wear this evening. Any coat will do."

Lambert looked at him a moment, then said, rather bluntly, "*Those* are words I never should have thought to have heard from them lips of yours! Just when, may I ask, did you become quite so draggletailed about your clothes, sir?"

"Since I came to this place, I think. Tell me, Lambert, are *you* enjoying yourself? *I'm* not! In fact, I can't remember ever having put up at a more dreary establishment."

"Well, I rather supposed the accommodations were not to your liking, sir."

"I'd be better off with the accommodations at a hedge tavern," muttered Hugh. "Lambert, is it my imagination or do you, too, get the distinct impression young Carville is done in at the knees?"

"I wouldn't venture to say, sir," responded his valet, diplomatically, "although I might hazard a guess this manor house has seen its better day."

Hugh ran a disapproving glance over the thin layer of dust that adorned each piece of furniture in his suite. It hadn't taken many moments after he and his friend, Lord Hetherington, had arrived at the Hall that Hugh had noticed that the place was furnished without the least elegance. "I rather think I agree with you. I might even go so far as to say that Carvington Hall is a trifle shabby."

"You'll find no argument from me, sir," said Lambert. He cast a hopeful look in his master's direction and ventured, "With arrangements such as these, I dare say no one should blame you if you and Lord Hetherington took it into your heads to leave first thing in the morning."

Hugh abandoned the pastoral scene outside the window and cast his valet an indulgent look. "No one, Lambert?"

His loyal servant interpreted this mild rejoinder as a sign of encouragement, and abandoned all pretense to diplomacy, saying, "Well, I wouldn't have the brains God gave a goose if I didn't see what's what, after all. I had my suspicions about the young lord 'afore we left London that he was living life on the nod. Then, when we finally arrive here, what do we find? Not one groom to look after your horses and no servant in the house but a female. I rather suspect *she* was the criminal responsible for the dog's din-

ner served up to us last night! From all I've seen since
we arrived here—If I dare be so bold to say—his young
lordship's pockets are stone cold.''

"Unnecessary to tell me!" said Hugh, who had been
provided ample opportunity to form such an opinion himself.

Lambert asked hopefully, "Were you thinking to leave,
sir? I dare say I can fetch some boys from the village to
put the horses to and we can be on our way to London
first thing in the morning."

"But we're not going to London," said Hugh, turning
back to the view outside his window. "My business is in
Bath."

"We might secure lodgings at a hotel in town, then,
sir," suggested Lambert. "You enjoyed your rooms at the
White Hart the last time we were in Bath, if I recall correct."

"I did, indeed, but I shall not be availing myself of
that establishment's hospitality on this occasion. We shall
remain here, at Carvington Hall."

Lambert's lips clamped into a thin line of disappointment. "Yes, sir," he said, after a moment. He held a coat
up and assisted his master in slipping his arms into the
sleeves and shrugging the garment up over his broad, muscled shoulders.

Hugh moved in front of the mirror, the better to survey
his appearance and adjust the immaculate white cuffs of
his shirt as they peeked from beneath his coat sleeves. In
the mirror he could see Lambert's image reflected behind
him, his back rigid with censure, a look of mulish mutiny
about his mouth.

"Something else, Lambert?"

"No, sir," muttered his valet through tight lips.

"Come, now! Give over and tell me what's put you in
such a mood."

Lambert, never one to refrain from speaking his mind

whenever such an opportunity presented itself, said promptly, "I should like to hear one good reason for us to remain here, in all the discomfort of this place, when in no more time than a pig's whisper we could be happily settled at the White Hart!"

"Because the White Hart will not serve my purpose. Hetherington and I have come here for one reason and one reason only: to earn a seat at Black Jack Hardy's card table. You know very well the man will never extend to either of us an invitation to his gaming party if he thinks I have pursued him to earn one. No, Hardy needs to believe that we are here on other business; he needs to be convinced that it is coincidence that causes his path and mine to cross. Remaining here at Carvington Hall is the perfect scheme. That way, when I meet him in town, I shall be able to tell Hardy, with perfect sincerity, that I am the guest of young Carville."

"I should imagine you would be better off being a guest of a London jailer," muttered Lambert. "There is not one servant in this place to attend to your needs, which means more work for me."

"Worried I shall wear you to the bone, are you?" asked Hugh, with some amusement.

"No, but I have been wondering how many trips I shall be required to make up those stairs with buckets of water when you announce you are ready for your bath," he retorted, impudently. "Or perhaps when you're ready for a fire to be lit in that hearth over there, you shall excuse the dirt and dust that shall cover me from head to toe once I'm finished cutting the kindling and carrying the coals up."

"I shall do my best to limit my demands upon you," said Hugh, mildly, but he was more affected by his valet's words than he was willing to allow. In fact, he was in complete agreement with Lambert's assessment of their accommodations at Carvington Hall. At one time the manor had probably been quite habitable, but to Hugh's fastidious eye, it was clear that the place had fallen on difficult times. He had detected no overt signs of penury, no patched carpets or ragged draperies, but he did notice a general pervasion of untidiness about the public rooms. In his own chamber, he was well aware that the paint on the walls was cracked and the bright colors of the carpets faded and bed linens well-worn.

"I imagine you shall," remarked Lambert, grudgingly, "but I hope you'll forgive my saying that it isn't like you to put up with such nonsense as we've encountered here. I dare say that if young Lord Carville were a man with more bronze, there might be something good to come of all this. But I've seen how the young lord follows after you with the look of a puppy about him and, now, to find the lad hasn't got a bean. Why, it's disgraceful!"

Again did Hugh agree with his valet's assessment; again did he refrain from saying so. Almost did Lambert convince him; almost was Hugh Deverill tempted to abandon his well-laid plans and leave Carvington Hall and its young, foolish owner far behind for a more accommodating suite of rooms at the White Hart. Almost did he consider that he had made a grave error in judgment just by accepting Carville's offer to stay a few days at the Hall. His expectations for his visit had been simple: the prospect of some excellent hunting and sufficient sport to fill his daylight hours, and some sparkling conversation with interesting fellow-guests in the evening, sprinkled throughout with just enough opportunities for some turns of the cards with deep-pocketed players to make the whole visit palatable.

But he and his friend, Hetherington, had arrived at Carvington Hall to discover Lord Carville's stables virtually empty, the house in mean condition, and themselves the only guests to a young host whose eagerness to please bordered on that of a toad-eater.

But a word from Carville, dropped in passing, that he had inherited a grand estate just outside Bath, had been enough for Hugh to decide to allow the acquaintance to continue. Having already heard that Jack Hardy, a rather high-rolling member of Watier's, had a house in Bath and intended to host there a card party of considerable stakes, Hugh needed to ensure that he, too, would be in Bath on the night the gaming would take place. It had taken little effort on his part to secure an invitation from Carville to stay; he had merely uttered some piece of nonsense about wishing to survey the countryside surrounding Bath. No further effort had been required; Carville had eagerly jumped at the chance to invite Hugh Deverill to sample life at Carvington Hall.

But that was before Hugh had been presented with proof of Carville's rather shoddy situation. No stately butler had greeted his arrival at the manor; no footmen had attended to his luggage. At dinner, his meal had been inedible; the wines, insipid; the cigars that followed, tasteless.

The entire situation was, Hugh decided, untenable. Much as he did not wish to do so, he knew that he could not remain any longer at Carvington Hall, and so he determined to tell his host that evening at dinner.

At the appointed hour he entered the dining room to find his host there before him. Moments later, Lord Hetherington entered, dressed splendidly in a waist coat of gold brocade and a coat of emerald velvet.

His host invited him to be seated. "Is it safe?" asked Lord Hetherington, inspecting his place setting with a suspicious eye.

Lord Carville laughed nervously. "Why? Do you think a bug might jump out at you?"

"My dear boy, that is the only discomfort that has not yet occurred since my arrival!"

He took his place at the dining table with great trepidation. Hugh sat down across from him, wondering himself what the evening might hold. Vividly did he recall the wretched repast that had comprised their dinner the night before and when Daisy appeared with trays bearing the first course, he braced himself for a repeat. On this night, however, his experience was on a different order. True, the meal that was set before him was a far cry from the usual *table d'hôte* he would have expected from the kitchens of an experienced chef. Yet his meal was decently prepared and was presented in an attractive manner that tempted his appetite to a certain degree; most importantly, the food was eminently edible.

Below stairs in the kitchens, Sara might have been gratified to have heard such cautious praise for her abilities, but she had been toiling too long and was nursing too deep an injury from her brother's treatment to give a thought to how well the meal she had prepared was being received by Philip and his guests.

By the time Daisy returned from serving the second course, Sara was feeling ill-used indeed. She had been away from home for almost two years; she had returned to find no welcome nor even a gig at the posting inn to meet her, and after having made her way home on her own, she had discovered that her only surviving relative, whom she had long adored and admired, was far from pleased to see her.

Daisy did her best to console her. "Well, now, miss, Lord Carville can't very well spend the evening with you when he's already invited his gentlemen friends to stay," she said, soothingly. She deposited on the table a tray full of dirty dishes she had collected from the dining room, and watched Sara arrange on another tray of silver the glasses and decanters of port to be sent up to the library.

"Why not?" demanded Sara. "He might have asked me to join them for dinner."

"Not with the language that's flying about that dining room!" said Daisy with authority.

Sara cast her a wide-eyed look. "Do you mean their language isn't fit for a lady's presence?"

"Well, I suppose that's how gentlemen speak, after all," Daisy said, reasonably. "And they do make an effort to hold their tongues as long as I'm in the room. But I did overhear them once as I was standing just outside the door, and I thought I would blush to the roots of my hair!"

"Why, that doesn't sound at all like Philip," said Sara with a puzzled frown. "Daisy, who *are* these men that they should have such an appalling influence over my brother?"

"I don't know their names, miss, but one of them is a lord and he's as fine as fivepence and just as pretty. I don't think I've ever seen a more beautiful man, miss, and that's the truth!"

Sara laughed. "Oh, Daisy, *men* are not beautiful!"

"This one is!" she insisted. "His hair is not as yellow as your brother's, miss, but it's just as pretty, with curls all about his head. And the jewelry, miss! I don't believe I've ever seen such a display of gold and jewels all at once on one person before!"

Sara laughed again. "He sounds quite fashionable! What about the other gentleman?"

"Oh, now, he's a cavey one, miss," said Daisy, her voice dropping to a covert tone. "A big man, he is, with eyes as cold and grey as a February sky!"

"Perhaps he's very pleasant once one gets to know him," offered Sara.

"I shouldn't think so," said Daisy, clearly doubtful. "The only time he shows any life is when I set a glass of spirits in front of him! Never speaks a word or smiles! Too high in the instep, if you ask me!"

"He does not at all sound like the sort of man Philip should invite into his home!" remarked Sara.

"More's the pity when anyone can see Lord Carville is striving so anxious to please him! His lordship should save his pains, for I get a rather bad feeling about that man. I wouldn't trust *that* London gentleman to be any more honorable than a nine quid note!" pronounced Daisy, as she pushed her way through the kitchen door with the tray of wines and glasses.

Sara was still puzzling over the validity of that characterization when Daisy returned to the kitchen moments later, with her hands flying in horror and the astonishing news that Sara had been summoned to the library.

"To the library!" Sara repeated. "Daisy, why would Philip want *me* to join them in the library?"

"It's not Lord Carville who insisted, but the pretty London gentleman, miss. He told Lord Carville he wanted to meet the chef responsible for tonight's dinner and Lord Carville told me to send Monsieur Henri up to them."

"But Henri didn't cook the dinner!"

"So I tried to say, but Lord Carville would have none of it! Closed his ears, he did, and told me to have his chef attend him straight away. What could I do, miss, when his lordship wouldn't listen to me? So I came straight to you!"

"Oh, dear! I had *hoped* they might have liked the dinner but I see now they did not! Daisy, what am I to do?"

"Truly, his lordship didn't appear to be angry, miss. Mostly I should guess it was the pretty gentleman who insisted upon making the chef's acquaintance."

Sara was far from encouraged. "Oh, dear! I knew I would have to tell Philip sooner or later that I've turned off his chef, but I would wish to do so in private," she said, anxiously. "I can only hope he may not be too vexed with me when he learns the truth!"

She needn't have worried, for at that moment Philip

Brandon-Howe, Viscount Carville, was feeling far from vexed. He had, in fact, consumed enough wine and port to have rendered him quite pleasantly foxed, leaving him with a sense of profound charity with the world. Having partaken of an excellent meal, he was comfortably settled in an overstuffed chair by the fire, and was engaged in parrying with befuddled good grace, the pointed and painful criticisms of his guest, Lord Hetherington.

"No, no, Carville!" said Lord Hetherington, his jeweled hand going up in laughing protest. "There is no point in arguing with me, no point at all! You, my young friend, have stepped into a puddle on this one; I agree with Deverill."

"B-but I'm telling you the truth, dash it!" said Philip.

"Impossible! I know French cooking, you impudent pup, and I shall never believe tonight's dinner was prepared by that great French chef you claim to have! What a colossal web of fiction you've spun, Carville! French chef, indeed!"

"But it's the truth, 'pon my honor!" insisted Philip. "I brought Henri down from London myself!"

Lord Hetherington gave his handsome head of golden curls a shake. "I shall never believe you have a Frenchman in the kitchen, even if you produced Bonaparte himself! Although, that's not to say the meal wasn't a far sight better than that prison fare you tried to serve us last night, wouldn't you say, Deverill?"

Mr. Hugh Deverill was standing in the shadows by the fireplace with one long arm draped negligently across the mantel and the stem of an empty wineglass twined between his extended fingers. He flicked a look of barely disguised annoyance toward Philip and considered that the time had come to inform his young host of his intention to depart in the morning.

He drained the last of the port from his glass and said in a low, measured voice, "The meal was, as you say, passable, but I fear it was not of a degree to tempt me to sample it again tomorrow night."

Philip bolted to his feet and grabbed a decanter from the side table. "Here, let me fill your glass for you, Deverill!" he said eagerly.

Watching his host perform that simple task put Lord Hetherington in mind of another complaint. "Where's your butler to pour out, Carville? Quite shabby, dear boy! Quite shabby! Not only have you no chef, but you've no servants, either! What the deuce did you do with them all?"

"Oh! Oh, there are servants, of course!" said Philip, weakly.

"Then you must be keeping them in a cupboard somewhere, for I swear I've seen not one servant except that maid who served us dinner tonight. Had it not been for the fact that I brought along my man and Deverill brought his valet and tiger, there would be no one to see to our needs at all." Lord Hetherington's aquiline nose wrinkled in distaste. "Quite shabby, Carville! Quite shabby, indeed!"

"Yes! Well, you're right, of course!" said Philip, trying to think clearly through the fumes of alcohol that fogged his brain. "I should have come down before your arrival to make sure everything about the place was ready. I—I never imagined to find my old home in a sorry state such as this!"

Lord Hetherington spoke again. "Really, Carville, someone must take you in hand! In the meantime, must *I* tell you everything you should do?"

"Yes!" said Philip, with the eagerness of one about to learn from a master.

"Very well!" he said, after a moment. "I've considered the matter and decided that you can have no better teacher than myself. But I simply cannot allow you to hang on my very elegant sleeve until you acquire a bit more bronze!

And some servants! I'm quite appalled that you haven't a housekeeper in a place of this size!"

Philip frowned. "A housekeeper?"

"Yes, dear boy! Someone to manage your household so *you* don't have to. A housekeeper will make sure the place is in readiness for your return at all times! I'm quite repulsed to find you haven't a chatelaine on your rolls!"

"Oh! A *chatelaine!* Of course I have a chatelaine," said Philip, quite willing to heap lie upon lie if it meant Lord Hetherington might look upon him with favor. "As it happens, I've just engaged one! Yes, indeed! I stopped in Bath on my way down from London and secured the services of a chatelaine! There is an agency in Bath, you see. Yes, a chatelaine! Yes, I've got one!" he finished lamely and with the frantic thought that he had no possible way of producing such a servant for his guests.

He was relieved to see that Lord Hetherington accepted this explanation easily as he helped himself to another glass of port. A glance at Mr. Hugh Deverill still lounging negligently against the mantelpiece, however, told Philip he had yet to earn that man's favor.

Philip was, by nature, a friendly young man, with a confident grace and impulsive smile that had always stood him in good stead. He had never before had trouble making friends of a man—until he met Hugh Deverill.

Philip had been in London, languishing amid some mighty dull company when Fortune had placed him in the path of Lord Hetherington. From there it had been a simple step to fall under the attention of Devil Deverill, whose acquaintance Philip cherished above all others for it opened to him a world to which he had long aspired and never dared hope to gain. He now had merely to tag after his new friends to know the heady thrill of entering Fives Court, or the dazzling prospect of blowing a cloud of smoke at The Daffy Club, or crossing the threshold of Gentleman Jackson's exclusive boxing school.

In the three weeks since Philip had entered Devil Deverill's select world of gaming hells, racing circuits, and exclusive card parties, Philip had done his very best to earn some measure of praise or acknowledgment from the man. His efforts were yet unrewarded.

Mr. Deverill's usual expression was one of reserve and Philip thought his manner was just as austere and formal as the exquisitely tailored coat he wore. He cut an imposing figure and Philip was anxious to engage him in some sort of conversation. But his consumption of wine made him incapable of forming any sparkling *bon mot* that might incite Mr. Deverill's admiration and the best he could at last contrive was to ask in a small voice, "I suppose you have a housekeeper in each of your houses, eh, Deverill?"

"Of course he does!" interjected Lord Hetherington. "Who else may we bachelors rely upon to make our lives beautiful and comfortable? Don't you agree, Deverill?"

"Naturally," said that gentleman in a colorless tone.

"You needn't rely merely on servants for your comfort, you know," said Philip, ingeniously.

"No?" countered Hugh with a rather quelling stare.

"You—you might take a wife!"

"Certainly," said Hugh. "Whose wife do you recommend?"

Philip was a good deal shocked by these words and regarded his guest in wide-eyed silence until he heard Lord Hetherington laugh aloud.

"Deverill, you dog!" his lordship exclaimed, still greatly amused. "Is it any wonder you're called Devil Deverill!"

"I'm known as Devil Deverill because *you* put the name about!"

"Then you have no one but me to thank for making you so notoriously fashionable!"

Philip, sparking under the excitement of this exchange, rolled an alert eye toward Hugh and waited for him to issue his usual crushing reply. Instead, he saw the briefest of smiles cross Hugh's face.

For a bare moment, the austerity of his expression softened and his grey eyes lit with a gleam of amusement. Then the smile was gone just as quickly as it had come, but Philip formed the instant opinion that he had been privileged to observe a rare event. He knew a sudden and certain swell of pride to think that by relaxing his rigid pose for a moment, Hugh Deverill might, perhaps, at last have granted him a place within his circle of intimates.

He joined in the laughter and was still grinning broadly when the door to the library opened and Sara entered the room. Philip bounded to his feet and regarded his sister with a confounded stare.

Sara paused just inside the library door, blushed rosily and regarded each gentleman with a look of innocent confusion.

She dipped a small curtsy and rose to find one of them moving toward her, appreciatively surveying her through his quizzing glass, and saying, "Upon my word! Carville, you dog, you swore to us there was not an eligible lady in the house! Shame on you for keeping such loveliness from us! I am Hetherington, my dear, very much at your service. And that great bulk by the mantel is Mr. Deverill. Do come in, my dear!"

From this introduction Sarah gathered the speaker was the young lord Daisy had mentioned.

"She's not loveliness and she's not eligible!" said Philip, finding his voice at last. He intercepted Sara and led her away from his guest's outstretched hand and back toward the door. "Sara, what *are* you doing here?" he demanded in a low and slightly slurred voice.

"I beg your pardon, but I am here to make a confession," she said quickly. "You see, I came upon Henri smashing the pottery and I *knew* you wouldn't condone such behavior! And poor Daisy was crying and the dishes were breaking and—and—" She stopped short, realizing that her nervous words were tumbling senselessly about. She took a deep, steadying breath and tried again. "What I'm trying to tell you is that *I* cooked your dinner tonight!"

Downstairs in the kitchens it had seemed such a simple matter to confess that she had turned off her brother's high-priced chef and had dared to substitute her own cooking for his. That was before she found Philip's blue eyes trained upon her with an expression of appalled horror.

"*You* cooked dinner? You're bamming me!" he said, with more astonishment than tact.

"You have been discovered, Carville!" exclaimed Lord Hetherington. "Wasn't it just as I said? French chef indeed!"

Sara clasped her hands together in a tight grip. "Please don't be angry, for I truly didn't mean to deceive you!"

Lord Hetherington stilled her nervous hands and drew her back into the room toward the fire.

"Nonsense, my dear! You quite mistake me for I was just telling Carville here that I very much fancied the way you prepared the foul. And your rhennish cream—a pure delight! But to believe the meal you put before us was the product of a great French chef as Carville claimed? No, that I could not quite bring myself to accept."

Sara relaxed visibly. "Thank you, sir! That is most kind of you. I enjoyed cooking the meal and I'm sure with a little more practice, I could become quite good at it."

Lord Hetherington regarded her for a startled moment, then he smiled. "Practice? Good at it? Oh, yes! How famous! I say, Carville, your cook has an enchanting sense of humor! Did you hear, Deverill?'' he asked, turning toward his friend.

He had, indeed, for his attention had been fixed upon Sara from the moment she had first entered the room. He was regarding her from his place at the mantel with an unfailing fixity that Sara considered most unnerving. But his voice, when he spoke, was quite colorless. ''Charming,'' he agreed, and he sketched a slight bow.

Lord Hetherington smiled happily upon her. ''She quite saves you, Carville, after you've dragged Deverill and me off to this shabby place of yours. I'm most displeased by your accommodations, you know. You've offered us no sport, no entertainment, and no servants to tend our needs. But if this fetching creature is to be your cook, I dare say there may be hope for you yet! She's a delight!''

Sara exchanged an astonished look with her brother, then said in a rather horrified voice, ''Oh, but sir! *I'm* not the cook! I mean, I did cook your dinner tonight, but— but I'm not the *cook!*''

She cast Philip a rather pleading look and found him staring back at her with an expression of bleary concentration. His cheeks were flushed and he was swaying slightly from the effects of his inebriated state but he still had enough of his wits about him to recognize an opportunity to show to advantage in front of his friends and repair a bit of the damaging opinion they had formed of him.

He fixed Sara with a very compelling look and said ruthlessly, ''No, she's not the cook. She's—she's the housekeeper! I told you I had engaged one, Hetherington, and, well, here she is!''

Chapter Three

For a moment Sara was too stunned to credit that she had heard her brother correctly. She could conceive of no reason he might say such a thing and she was about to demand, in affronted tones, an explanation for his singular behavior when she caught the minatory gleam in his eye.

He clasped her by the elbow and propelled her back toward the door. "I told you I had engaged a *chatelaine*, Hetherington!" he said, as he gave the skin of her forearm a premonitory pinch before he released her. "I dare say she'll have everything in order in no time and you'll find my hospitality quite to your liking in future!"

The awful scowl Philip directed toward his sister warned her not to argue and only added to her bewilderment. Nervously, she glanced at the other two gentlemen and saw Lord Hetherington watching her with an expression of good-natured interest. Mr. Deverill, on the other hand, levered his broad shoulders against the mantel and straightened to his full height, all the while watching her keenly. He stepped out of the shadows by the mantel and into the light in the center of the room and Sara had her first clear look at him.

Until that point, Sara's realm of experience with men had been limited to those gentlemen who comprised her brother's young circle of friends. Still, she knew a handsome man when she saw one, and she certainly could detect in him a style of the first elegance. No man she had ever met cut such an elegant figure as Hugh Deverill. His coat fit as if it had been molded to his shoulders, and his waistcoat, of muted green brocade, was an exquisitely tailored garment that somehow accentuated. He was not overly tall, but his presence was imposing, and his legs were muscular and shapely.

She had a sudden notion that his expression had undergone a change when first she had entered the room, and he now stood regarding her with a look of appraising interest.

Philip recalled her attention, saying, in a low, rather slurred voice, "Just do as I say, and don't contradict me, won't you? I swear, Miss Sassy, I shall make it worth your while!"

He had meant his words for Sara's ears only, but the amount of wine he had consumed had clouded his judgment on all fronts. Certainly, Hugh Deverill overheard his remarks for he said, "As shall I make it worth your while, young lady, if you will say again, in a clear, strong voice, that it was you who cooked our dinner tonight, and not some French chef."

"I have already told you so," said Sara, feeling rather nervous and a trifle bewildered. "I admit everything! It was I who cooked your dinner."

"I thank you, Miss—Miss Sassy? No, I refuse to believe that is your name, even though I overheard Carville call you so. Tell me, what is your name? I merely wished to thank you for making me richer by the sum of one-hundred pounds.''

"Did I do that?" she asked. "How?"

"By winning for me a bet I made with your employer over the dinner table. Pay up, Carville."

Sara looked from Mr. Deverill to her brother and back again. "But I don't understand. What was the bet?"

"Your employer assured both me and Hetherington that our dinner had been prepared by a French chef. I contended otherwise and thanks to your confession, I have been proven correct."

Sara's eyes widened as she regarded Philip. "A hundred pounds? Why, that's a small fortune!"

"Oh, now, don't fly up in the boughs, Sara," said Philip, dampeningly. "After all, wagering is something men do on a fairly regular basis. You wouldn't understand such things!"

"I understand only that you have lost a hundred pounds over a silly dinner!" she retorted, losing the last of her patience.

Lord Hetherington's smile grew. "Your housekeeper is quite charming! Such spirit! She's a breath of fresh air, Carville!"

"I am not any of those things," said Sara. She was fast wondering how things had come to such a bewildering pass. She looked at her brother and said, half-demanding, half-pleading, "Tell them who I am!"

"I've already done so," said Philip, mulishly. "You're the housekeeper; the one I hired from an agency in Bath." He made another attempt to escort her to the door and found that this attempt was much more successful than the last. At the door, he leaned toward her and whispered, quite urgently, "Please! Don't ask any more questions and don't contradict me. It's important, Sara. Please!"

These words, accompanied by a look of frantic purpose,

convinced Sara that her brother was embroiled in some sort of fix. She didn't understand what exactly was going on, but she wasn't about to turn him down in his time of need.

She whispered back, "Very well—if it's important!" and saw a great deal of the strain vanish from his expression.

Philip closed the library door upon her then, and Sara was left alone in the hall, plagued with a score of unanswered questions concerning his uncommon behavior. That he had been drinking, she had no doubt. That he had told his guests a score of falsehoods was obvious. She wasn't at all sure she could fathom the reason for his having done so, but she strongly suspected Mr. Deverill had something to do with Philip's misconduct.

Sara never had an opportunity to question her brother that night. She was fast asleep long before he and his house guests quitted the library and made their ways to their separate chambers, but upon waking the next morning, she was more determined than ever to have words with her brother.

She donned a simple morning dress of muslin and tied her golden brown curls on top of her head with a plain ribbon of blue that matched her eyes, and set off for the hall to lay in wait for Philip.

Her vigil was a long one. The clock in the great entry room had chimed only nine times when she took up her position there. In the end, it chimed many more times before she at last caught a glimpse of her brother. In vain did she listen for the sounds of anyone else astir the house, and she began to pace idly about the hall. Her observant eye caught site of the gloves and hat Philip had left behind on a table the night before. She picked these items up, and immediately noticed the marks they left in the dust on the table top.

For the first time since her return home, Sara took a

critical look about her and was rather shocked to realize that the warm, richly appointed great hall of her memory resembled not at all the room she now saw. The hall was dim and uninviting, and the parquetry floors were faded and noticeably worn. The carpets were threadbare and the brass sconces and door hinges had grown tarnished and dingy. To a casual visitor, the state of Carvington Hall might seem a trifle unkempt, but to Sara, nothing could have been worse than to see her beloved home in such a state of utter shabbiness.

She was still inventorying the sad appearance of the hall when she heard a man's deep voice behind her, saying, "Good morning!"

Startled, Sara turned and found Mr. Hugh Deverill looking down upon her from the first landing of the grand staircase. She dipped a small curtsy and watched him descend the stairs with the natural grace of an athlete. Upon making his acquaintance the night before, Sara had thought him a good-looking man; in the early hours of a June morning, he was a dashing figure to behold. He was dressed for riding, in boots and buckskins and a coat of exceptional cut that fitted so well across his shoulders that she wondered that he could move his arms.

In one hand he carried his riding hat, with his crop tucked under his arm; in his other hand was a pair of tan leather gloves of exquisite workmanship that had, she was sure, cost the earth.

Slowly, Sara's blue eyes traveled up and met his, encountering a look of mild amusement. For the barest of moments, with her blue eyes locked in communion with his grey ones, she felt a faint pull of attraction. Mr. Hugh Deverill, she thought, was a man who undoubtedly excited admiration wherever he went; many a feminine heart undoubtedly beat a good deal faster whenever he chanced to look upon a woman in just that way. She knew hers certainly did.

He said, as he reached the bottom step, "I hope I didn't startle you, just now, Miss—Miss—I refuse to believe your name is 'Sassy!' "

Sara was forcibly reminded of the folly of her brother's lie and was sorely tempted to right Mr. Deverill's notion of her position in the house. Only a deep, abiding affection for her brother caused her to say, with tight constraint, "You are correct, sir. I believe Lord Carville told you my name."

"No, he didn't. But I did hear him call you 'Sara,' I think. Am I to do the same? No, don't poker up at me. I like you better when you are not hiding behind a housekeeper's impassivity. Tell me, then, if I'm not to call you Sara, what *am* I to call you?"

Sara did not at all know how to reply to such a question. She had not yet had an opportunity to discover from Philip his reasons for having told such tales and lies as he had last night in the library; surely he had done so only for good reason and she didn't want to say the wrong thing and somehow make his matters worse. She turned away slightly, and said, "Sir, I am merely the housekeeper."

"You are nothing like any housekeeper I ever chanced to come across—and I assure you, I've come across a great many!"

"Are you as coming with them as you are with me?" she asked, in a disapproving tone.

"Oh, no, for you are the prettiest of the lot, you see," he answered promptly.

She didn't know whether to be pleased or vexed; she was certainly disarmed and felt the heat of a blush cover her cheeks. She tried to dispel any feelings of embarrassment by changing the subject: "Will—will your friend be joining you for your morning ride?"

"Hetherington? I doubt it; he needs his beauty rest. Besides, it is a rule among true men of fashion that one never rises before noon, no matter what the occasion."

She blinked at him. "But aren't *you* a true man of fashion?"

"Yes, but I like to make my own rules. Tell me, how long have you worked for Carville?"

"How—how long?" It was a question she had not anticipated and she truly had no notion how to reply. If she admitted to employment of short duration, she was fearful Philip should be stigmatized as a flat, unable to employ a sufficient number of servants to run his household. On the other hand, if she confessed to being employed for a longer term, she ran the risk of incurring Mr. Deverill's criticism for allowing the manor to fall into such shabby repair.

She decided to avoid his question altogether, saying, "Well, let me see . . . goodness, why do you wish to know?"

"No reason. I simply enjoy making conversation with pretty housekeepers."

"Indeed? Then I hope you may find one who enjoys it as much as you. Perhaps while you are riding this morning you shall come across a housekeeper on horseback who shall chatter your ear off. Good morning, Mr. Deverill!"

"Dismissing me, are you?" he asked, his good nature unimpaired. "Very well, I shall leave you to your inspection of the front hall, but I should warn you that it's very likely our paths shall cross again. Next time, you may not be able to fob me off with such a charming snub."

She hadn't meant to be charming; in fact, she had hoped to insult the man enough that he would be abused of any desire to engage her attention in the future. The smile he cast her as he left the hall dashed such hopes.

Hugh Deverill, she thought, was not at all a man who was used to meeting with rebuffs, especially from a female.

He was, most likely, an accomplished flirt, and Sara's refusal to play at his game was no doubt, she thought, a novel experience for him. She was, however, not a vindictive person, and she had no wish to hurt him or wound his pride; she merely wished him otherwise. In her judgment, his manner was a bit too polished to be trusted, and his smile, much too charming to be enjoyed. Other than that, he was a handsome specimen of a man. Almost Sara might have been dazzled by a man so well-favored in face and form had she not observed with her own eyes just last evening, evidence that his character was less than sterling.

In the library she had been convinced of his influence over Philip—an influence that was far from beneficial. With cool indifference he had tricked Philip into wagering what seemed to Sara an exorbitant sum. Judging by the state of Carvington Hall and the lack of funds left to maintain it, Philip was making it a practice to hand over fists full of cash to Mr. Deverill. Well, no more!

And so Sara determined to tell her brother as soon as he emerged from his bedchamber. That event, however, remained a long time in coming; she waited almost another hour, and still Philip did not appear.

With sisterly impatience Sara climbed the stairs and entered Philip's chamber only to find the drapes still drawn, the room still dark, and its sole occupant fast asleep in the soft depths of his four-poster bed.

Sara threw back the draperies and, finding that even the light of a bright June morning was not enough to cause Philip to stir, she picked up a pillow from where it had fallen on the floor and gave it a mighty swipe in his direction.

He awoke with a start, and sat up immediately, his eyes unfocused and his hair tousled from sleep. "What the devil!"

Sara swung the pillow at him again, and this time she

had the satisfaction of pelting him in the face with it. "Wake up!" she commanded, ready to launch another attack. "Wake up, you rotter, and tell me what you meant by treating me so last night!"

Philip moved suddenly to dodge the flying pillow and was quickly and forcibly reminded how much wine he had consumed the night before. He raised his arm to fend off the blow, saying, "Oh, my head! Leave off, for God's sake! What kind of a bee has got into your bonnet?"

"Never mind bees—*you* are to blame for this! How dare you tell your guests I am your housekeeper!" demanded Sara, with deep emotion. "I was never more shocked! I dare say you would never have told such a whisker if you hadn't been stabbed in the neck!"

"You mean *shot* in the neck, you ridiculous bagpipe, and stop hitting me!" He wrestled the pillow from her with little effort. Propping it up against the headboard, he leaned back against it and frowned at her. "Is that what's got your toga in a knot?—that I told Deverill and Hetherington you were the housekeeper?"

"Of course it is!" she said, crossly, "and I'll thank you not to speak of it so casually. Of all the insufferable tricks!"

"I suppose you're right," said Philip, running a hand through his hair. "I should never have said it, but I was in a damnable bind, you know, what with Deverill threatening to leave and Hetherington reading me a curtain lecture as if I were nothing but a pup. Perhaps it was the brandy fumes talking, but I'm—I'm sorry, Sara!"

She had never been able to maintain her anger whenever he adopted just such a tone. The irritation immediately drained from her expression and she said, rather gently, "I know you are. Now it only remains that you confess to both gentlemen that you lied and tell them I am not your housekeeper, after all."

Philip frowned. "Here now, why should I do that?"

"Because—because you must make it right, Philip."

"Don't be daft! I can't tell men like Devil Deverill and Jasper Hetherington that there are no servants to be had in my home! They expect me to have a butler and footmen and a—a—what the devil did he call it? A *chatelaine!*"

Sara's temper rose. "But you haven't a butler and you haven't a footman, Philip. Most importantly, you haven't a *chatelaine!* Simply tell them so!"

"Well, if you ain't the biggest social idiot I ever met," he retorted, in disgust. "Don't you know who Devil Deverill is? He's a regular dash, that's what! And I've worked too hard to earn his notice to have you spoil it for me now!"

"I saw nothing to recommend him," challenged Sara. "In fact, quite the opposite! I find I cannot like him at all!"

"That's all you know! Any man who can control the kind of prime cattle Devil Deverill takes in hand must be a capital fellow. Sara, you'll never guess! He draws his curricle with three matched greys. Three! Did you ever?"

"Indeed?" she countered, with stunning hauteur. "I have been told his reputation is as dishonest as a nine-quid note!"

Philip shot her a smoldering look. "Nice! Very nice, indeed! Is that the kind of language they taught you at that school?"

It had been a far from gracious remark, and Sara knew it, but she wasn't about to apologize to her brother over her own ill-judged words when he was guilty of uttering even greater atrocities. "Never mind *my* language," she said, drawing herself up. "Are you going to tell those gentlemen the truth or are you not?"

"For God's sake, Sara, do you know what you're asking?" he demanded, exasperated. "A man like Deverill—why, it was a great piece of luck and finagling that led him to accept my invitation to even come here—*here,* to Carv-

ington Hall! Sara, you cannot conceive what an honor it
is to be singled out so!''

"Next you shall tell me the man walks on water!''

"He does among the Corinthian set!" rejoined Philip.
"I've spent a small fortune polishing myself and putting
myself in the way for him to notice me, and I'll not have
all my efforts go for naught now that I've contrived to get
the man in my own home!''

Sara looked at him for a long moment before asking
quietly, "Is that where all the money has gone, then? Is
that why there are no servants left and the manor has fallen
into such a state?''

"Well, the truth of the matter is, our father didn't cut
up as warm as I thought he would.''

Sara digested this information as she slowly sat down
upon the bed beside her brother. After a thoughtful
moment she said, solemnly, "Then it's true. We *are* poor!''

"Yes, but only for a little while," replied Philip, optimisti-
cally. "I dare say we can survive on our quarter-day allow-
ances until our fortunes are repaired.''

"How, may I ask, are we to repair our fortunes?''

He ran the back of his fingers down her cheek in a
brotherly expression of affection. "Leave that to me, Miss
Sassy, if you please! In the meanwhile, we must only remain
on Deverill's good side. If he were to turn his back on me,
I should be ruined and all my efforts—everything I've
worked for—shall be for naught!''

Sara gave her head a slight shake. "I cannot like him,
Philip.''

"You don't have to like the man. God's teeth, Sara, I'm
not asking you to marry him; I just want his room clean!''

"But, can I not run the household and still be your
sister?" she pressed.

"But I've already told Deverill and Hetherington you're
the housekeeper. Please, Sara! Only think of it as when we

were children, dressing up and pretending to be someone other than we were. You'll see! It will be a lark. We'll laugh about it later, mark my words!''

"But—but a *housekeeper!*" she said, clearly reluctant.

"Only for two days. They'll be gone then—bound for London, I should guess—and you'll never have to see them again. My oath on it!''

It was a difficult thing for Sara to resist her brother whenever he employed that coaxing tone. Since the first time she had set out to tag after him on one of his childish adventures, Sara had never failed to bend to Philip's imperious will. She could not like the scheme, but she was not prepared to do more battle with him over visitors that would be gone forever within two days time.

She looked at him a moment, then said, with little good grace, "Very well!''

"I knew you'd come about! There's a girl!" commended Philip, brightening. "Now, if only you can contrive to *look* like a housekeeper! You can't very well dress as you are now, you know.''

Sara looked down at her fashionable muslin gown and made a face. "I suppose I might wear the grey and black frocks I wore in mourning, but I shall not look well in them!''

"You'll look as right as wax. You always do! Besides, it doesn't matter how you look, as long as you can arrange to have some decent food set before us! If you can contrive to feed us for the remaining meals as well as you did last night, we won't starve!''

Sara jumped up from the bed, saying, "Oh, no! *I* don't intend to do the cooking. I shall keep your house, Philip, but I shall *not* cook!''

The smile fell quickly from his lips. "What do you mean?''

"I mean I shall supervise the preparation of meals, but

I won't prepare them myself. Goodness, did you really suppose I spent the better part of the last two years at Miss Pembleton's school just so I could toil in a kitchen?"

"Well, who, then, is going to do it if you don't, I should like to know? We can't very well starve nor will I let Daisy try her best to poison us again!"

"I shall engage a cook," said Sara, quite calmly. "I shall go into Bath this morning and hire a cook from an agency."

"Of all the—! Haven't you been listening? I haven't the rhino to hire a legion of servants."

"But I have. I have a bit of the money left from my last quarter-day and I think if I am careful and not extravagant, I should be able to manage very nicely. I mean to go to Bath and engage not only a cook, but another maid and a footman, as well. And I shall take your bills and accounts right now, Philip, so I may visit each shop and pay something against the amounts you owe."

"We owe," interpolated Philip.

She ignored this sally and, moving toward the door, said, "If I am to play the part of your housekeeper, you must promise to allow me to handle the accounts from now on."

"You?" repeated Philip, deeply affronted. "May I remind you that *I* am the head of this family?"

"You may be the head of this family, but *I* am the head of this household," said Sara, with a decided gleam in her blue eyes, "and the household accounts fall under the domain of the *chatelaine.*"

"Well, if you don't turn colors faster than anything on this earth!" he remarked in a wondrous tone.

Sara smiled sweetly back. "We have a bargain, you and I. In return for playing the part of a housekeeper, you shall allow me to enjoy all the privileges that attend that position. From now on, *I* shall keep the household accounts, Philip. Fair is fair, after all!''

"Oh, is it? Is it, now?" demanded Philip and he took up the pillow from the bed and playfully launched it through the air, straight toward Sara.

"Oh!" cried Sara, as the pillow hit her square upon the side of her head. Turning, she saw Philip select another pillow from his arsenal of cushions on the bed.

With a rompish squeal, Sara yanked the door open and scampered out into the corridor just as Philip sent the second pillow flying. The pillow hit the heavy oak door; the door slammed into her back like a cannon ball, propelling her into the hallway, straight into the arms of Mr. Hugh Deverill.

Finding his arms suddenly filled with housekeeper, Hugh did the only thing a man of sound constitution and healthy libido could do under the circumstance: he tightened his hold about Sara.

Chapter Four

For a moment both Sara and Hugh were too stunned to react at all; then Hugh instinctively adjusted his hold, molding her soft, lithe body intimately against his. "Well, this is a surprise!" he murmured.

A surprise, indeed. For a moment Sara could hardly think. She was aware only of the unexpected feeling of his warm breath dancing softly against her ear and she felt his chin rub against the curls that adorned the top of her head. With insouciant ease he pressed her yielding form against his steely length; his arms, like bands, continued to encircle her.

Sara couldn't think what to do; her heart was thundering in a way she was sure had nothing to do with the exertion of dodging Philip's aim with a pillow. Then she made the mistake of looking up at him, into his grey eyes that held within their depths a hint of gentle amusement.

A rush of heat mantled her cheeks and she gave an ineffectual push against the muscled wall of his chest. "I—

I beg your pardon!'' she said, in a voice of deep confusion. "I didn't realize—! I should never have—! Oh, my goodness!'' She stopped short, furious at her own incoherence.

Through every last word of her stammered speech, Hugh continued to regard her with bland amusement. She pushed against him once more, again without result; then slowly, as if he were loath to release her, he relaxed his arms a bit.

"No need to apologize, madam," he said, still reluctant to give her her freedom. "Mine is the blame for not having anticipated such a collision."

He glanced toward the heavy, paneled door, wondering what in blue blazes might have occurred behind it to have sent a housekeeper dashing through its portal. Then he realized that standing on the other side of the door was the bedchamber of none other than the master of Carvington Hall.

In an instant did he recall the moment he had found his arms full of her: her blue eyes had been bright and her full, soft lips had been parted in a happy smile. Her hair remained somewhat tousled and her escape from the bedchamber had been punctuated with a squeal of girlish delight.

So! Young Lord Carville was on rather intimate terms with his lovely young housekeeper, was he? No wonder he had kept her hidden and out of sight when first they had arrived at the Hall. Hugh couldn't blame him for that; the girl was a delight. Fresh and sweet-natured, with a young, trim body that moved with a surprisingly elegant rhythm— she was, in short, enchanting, and exactly what he needed to liven up the dismally dull accommodations he was being forced to endure.

A mild flirtation, a simple seduction, and Hugh considered that he just might find a way to end his stay at Carvington Hall with some pleasant memories after all. Surely young Carville wouldn't object; nor would the young lady. Hugh knew he had much more to offer her than an early morning roll on the bed, apparently what she was accustomed to getting from Carville.

"You are still touching me!" she hissed in an accusing tone that recalled his attention.

"So I am." He let her go then, and watched her take a few wary steps back until she was well out of reach of his arms. "I like the way your hair smells."

Now thoroughly disarmed, Sara tried to assume the rigid pose of a dispassionate employee. "It is not right that you would speak to me so," she said, clasping her hands together and drawing herself up to her full height. "Perhaps it will be easier for you to remember my position, sir, once I have served you your breakfast."

He had a rather good idea what position he should like her to be in, but he refrained from saying so. He said, instead, "No breakfast for me, madam. I have business to attend. I hope, however, I shall have the pleasure of colliding with you in another corridor very soon."

He bowed ever so politely, and continued on his way in the direction of his own chamber, leaving Sara behind to fervently pray the occasion should never arise when she would have to cross paths with him again.

She didn't care to feel confused and she disliked being breathless; Mr. Hugh Deverill had the power to exact both effects upon her. She was inexperienced in the art of flirtation, but she had a strong suspicion that she had just been the recipient of Mr. Deverill's considerable charm. To what purpose he had singled her out to receive his attentions, she could not guess; to what end he hoped their relationship would go was beyond her power to reason.

She knew only that she was considerably uncomfortable whenever he was about and she rather thought it a good idea to avoid his presence for the next two days until his departure.

That, she knew, would not be a difficult task, for she had already planned to dedicate all her time toward setting Carvington Hall back to rights. In her own bedchamber she donned pelisse, bonnet, and gloves and prepared to go into Bath.

Daisy had already apprised her of the fact that most of the carriages and horses had been sold off long ago, leaving only a few of Philip's hunters in the stables. Those animals, she knew, were most unsuitable to slip between the rails of a gig. Since her shoes were sturdy and her pelisse quite warm, she didn't think she would mind walking the few short miles into Bath.

Sara had not ventured very far down the road when she heard the sounds of a vehicle approaching from the direction in which she had come. She moved over to the side of the narrow road, the better to allow driver and equipage a sufficient portion of road in which to pass. Too late did she realize that the vehicle that was drawing to a halt beside her was a very elegant sporting curricle, and that Mr. Hugh Deverill was in possession of the reins.

He presented such a picture of graceful competence that Sara had little trouble understanding how her brother could be so keen on him. His was truly a dashing figure, exquisitely clothed, and riding in a graceful curricle drawn by a high-couraged pair of matched bays that Sara judged had probably sent sporting-mad Philip into a frenzy of admiration the first time he had set eyes on them.

His tiger leapt gracefully down and ran to the horses' heads as Hugh touched his gloved hand to the brim of his hat, saying, "This is Fate, I think! If you are going into Bath, I should be happy to drive you."

All the feelings of deep disorder Sara had suffered earlier that morning in the hallway came back to her in one rushing wave. Primly, she clasped her hands together and said, "Thank you, I prefer to walk!"

He put up one eyebrow. "Afraid?"

"Certainly not!" she retorted. "I merely prefer to enjoy a morning exercise."

"Come, come! I don't know what business you have in Bath, but you cannot arrive with your cheeks flushed and your hair blown about. I find those effects quite charming, I assure you, but the town tabbies shall not." He stretched down his hand to her, but still she hesitated. "I promise not to molest you, if that's any help in deciding it."

"Of course not! I never—I mean, I didn't think—! Oh!" uttered Sara, once again confused by his direct gaze and disconcerting words.

Unable to think of any suitable excuse to decline his invitation, Sara lifted her skirts in one hand and held the other up to him. He grasped it and easily pulled her up onto the seat beside him. They were off in an instant, and Sara felt the little curricle lurch slightly as the tiger swung himself up behind.

Too late did Sara discover the treachery of a simple curricle; the narrowness of the bench seat required that Sara sit quite close upon him. With every slap of the reins on the horses' backs, Hugh's well-muscled arm rubbed against hers; with every flick of his driving whip, Sara grew more vividly conscious of his nearness.

She sat rigidly upright beside him, her eyes firmly fixed upon the road, lest her gaze should stray toward the thick strength of his buckskin-clad thighs stretched out before him.

Hugh, on the other, remained quite at his ease and, despite the speed at which he drove his vehicle, he managed to apply a certain amount of attention to her profile.

"Do you know, you have remarkable eyes?" he said, in a conversational tone that still managed to make her jump.

"They are quite the loveliest eyes I have ever seen. I would hazard a guess that in your case, it is true what they say about the eyes being a mirror to a soul."

Sara's back went stiff as a plank. "I would be grateful if you did not speak to me so! I had hoped you would be enough of a gentleman not to take advantage of my driving with you."

"I can't very well take advantage of you with my tiger riding up behind," said Hugh, mildly. "He's a very excellent chaperone. You may trust him, I think."

"Trust him? I—I don't even know him!"

"That's remedied easily enough. Let me introduce to you my tiger, Jim Cotton. Jim, this is Lord Carville's housekeeper. Feel free to cuff me if you observe that my behavior toward this young woman crosses the line!"

"It will be my pleasure, sir," said Jim Cotton, "and I shall try not to hurt you too badly."

"There! You are most thoroughly protected!"

"And you are quite ridiculous," she said, trying to sound severe, but failing.

"Excellent! I was hoping I might have the pleasure of seeing you smile at least once. Very well, I shan't tease you anymore and I promise I shall be on my best behavior. Tell me, how old are you?"

Startled, her eyes flew to his face. "I—is that your idea of best behavior? To ask how old I am?"

"Evasive, but at least you didn't lie. Remember what I said about your eyes—I'll always know if you are less than truthful with me. So you want to keep your age a secret! Very well! Tell me instead, then: is Lord Carville merely your employer or have you any more binding ties to him?"

By now truly alarmed, Sara's wide eyes flew to his, fearful that he should have guessed that she was not what she presented herself to be. She encountered no light of suspicion in his expression but that afforded her little peace.

With every new question, she thought, Hugh's voice became more hypnotic, more seductive. And with every answer, Sara felt more unsure, more nervous and breathless.

She tried to parry his last inquiry with a tremulous laugh. "Sir! Such—such questions as you ask me!"

"How many times have you been kissed, Sara?"

Too stunned for a moment to answer, Sara realized she was entering murky waters, indeed. She should have scolded him; she should have demanded that he stop the curricle so she might leap to the ground, abandoning his escort in disgust, but his last query had left her feeling confused and disarmed and unable to think clearly. Certainly, the first question he had posed was much easier to answer, and much less threatening. She had an incoherent notion that she might distract him by answering his first question now, and uttered, "Nineteen!"

His grey eyes widened with a mixture of surprise and amusement. "Indeed? *Nineteen?* Tell me, madam, what could have possessed you to count?"

She looked uncomfortably out across the passing scenery, feeling flustered and foolish. In a strangled voice, she said, "My—my employer!"

Hugh was quiet a moment, his expression blank; then a light of recognition cleared his brow. "I suppose I *could* ask that you kindly answer my questions at the time in which they are put to you, but I think your way is much more entertaining. Let me see if I have this right: you are nineteen years old, are you not?" He received no more answer than a nod. "And I believe you next answered my second question and admitted that Lord Carville is merely your employer and nothing more?"

"Of-of course!"

He cast her his most charming smile. "Never let it be said that Hugh Deverill has difficulty communicating with the fairer sex! I believe we understand each other at last—except for my last question, of course. I don't suppose you would care to answer it now?''

Ever rigid, Sara shook her head. "No, sir, I-I would not!''

He laughed. "Very well! Your experience with kisses shall remain a mystery—for the time being, at least! Let us find some more innocent topic of conversation: perhaps you could tell me instead, what business takes you to Bath?''

Almost she breathed a deep sigh of relief at the change in subject, and answered, most promptly, "I am on a mission to hire servants for Carvington Hall. And you, sir? What business takes you to town?''

"Acquaintances. I am interested in knowing if one in particular has made his way to Bath for the summer. His name is John Hardy; have you ever heard of him?''

She shook her head. "I am not familiar with Bath society. Mr. Hardy must be a particularly good friend of yours to make you so anxious to see him.''

"Friend? No—gull, more like. He thinks himself quite the sharp at cards. He even calls himself, Black Jack Hardy. He put word about that he was removing to Bath for the summer and might consider hosting a gaming party one evening. I intend to be seated at the table when the cards are dealt.''

Sara looked up at him in some surprise. "Do you mean to tell me, you traveled all the way to Bath from London for a simple card party?''

"Simple? You wrong me! There is, in fact, a certain amount of skill involved in which I take much pride.''

"You called Mr. Hardy a gull. I'm well aware of that term; you think him a poor card player, someone from whom you shall be able to win a lot of money. That is your intent!''

"That is my vocation,'' he answered, amiably.

"Vocation? What a lovely term for taking advantage of another!"

He looked at her a moment, noting her heightened color, and said, with infinite patience, "I don't gamble with children, Sara, only with men capable of thinking for themselves. Every man who sits down at a baize-covered table is well-aware that he has as good a chance of losing money as winning."

"And how much money has my—has Lord Carville lost, I wonder?" she asked, casting him a burning look.

"To others? I do not know. To me? Quite a bit."

He saw her look away for a moment and presently, when she turned back so he could once again see her face, he saw, quite clearly, that she was troubled.

"Why do you ask? Are you concerned Carville hasn't the lolly to pay your wages? That, I'm afraid, is a matter you must address with him."

"There is no need to do so, I assure you!" she said, smarting from the callousness of his remark. "Pray, do not busy yourself over my wages or anything else about my employment at Carvington Hall!"

"I don't intend to, but I might busy myself over you," said Hugh mildly. "No, don't poker up at me. I promised I wouldn't take advantage of you and I usually make it a habit to keep my promises . . . for the time being, at least. Ah, we approach Bath. Tell me where your business takes you so I may drop you."

"I am bound for Milsom Street, but please don't think you must drive me there," said Sara, feeling anxious, indeed, to be set down from the curricle and be gone at last from Mr. Deverill's side.

He cast her a sidelong look of mild amusement. "I shall drop you wherever you are bound. Believe me, your destination is not out of my way, and besides, it does me a great deal of credit to be seen driving with a pretty woman."

He negotiated the turn onto Milsom Street, and asked, "Do you know the number you are seeking?"

"No. I know only that there is a domestic agency somewhere in Milsom Street. I assure you, if you will only pull up and set me down, I shall find it easily enough."

"You might," said Hugh, as he reined in his horses at the next corner, "or you might find yourself walking several miles. There's no need when we might very easily ask directions."

The curricle came to a stop. Jim Cotton jumped down from his perch behind, saying, "If you can hold them bays of yours, sir, I shall just ask after Madam's destination in that haberdashery there."

Jim disappeared into the shop and emerged a few moments later with the intelligence that there was, indeed, an agency for domestics a few doors down.

"A short stroll shouldn't be too strenuous, I should think," said Hugh. He tossed the reins to Jim Cotton and leapt gracefully down to the flagway. "Hold the horses, Jim, and walk them if you have to. I'll escort Miss Sara safely to her destination."

Sara looked down to find Hugh holding his hand expectantly up to her. She hesitated only a moment before allowing him to help her down, but she said, as soon as her feet were solidly fixed upon the ground, "There is no need for you to accompany me, I assure you, Mr. Deverill!"

"Trying to be rid of me, Sara?" he asked, quietly.

Utterly disarmed, she realized she should have anticipated his saying something quite disconcerting but instead she found herself stammering in reply. "Certainly not! It is only—I shouldn't wish to keep you! Surely you have business to attend to! I have, after all, only a short distance to walk!"

"Yes, but you cannot walk it alone and unescorted."

"I assure you, I can. I am, after all, a simple house-keeper!"

"You don't look like a housekeeper," said Hugh, clasping her gloved hand and fitting it within the crook of his elbow. He established a slow, leisurely walking pace that Sara had no choice but to follow. "In fact, there is nothing about you at all that resembles a servant. If that much is apparent to me, it is certainly apparent to other passersby. You need an escort if you wish to walk the streets of Bath. For now, that escort will be me."

They walked some distance in silence, before Sara asked, in a burning tone, "*Why* can I not walk unescorted in Bath?"

"Because young ladies do not do so."

"But I've already told you: I am merely a housekeeper."

"And I've already told you: you don't *look* like a house-keeper. You look like a young lady of fashion—at least, you certainly fit the height and figure requirements of a grown young woman. Besides, your pelisse is quite modish and the bonnet you are wearing, despite being of a style that is usually worn by schoolgirls, is handsomely trimmed and frames your face quite fetchingly. In short, you do not look like a housekeeper or any other servant one would care to name."

She didn't know whether to be flattered or offended by his observations. She said, in case there were any last doubt, "But I assure you, I *am* the housekeeper of Carvington Hall!"

"So you have told me—too many times, I think. Tell me, wouldn't you rather stroll the streets of Bath in search of treasures than domestic help? Only look at that shop window and the trinkets displayed there!"

They stopped in front of the large display window of one of Bath's most fashionable shops. There were, indeed, some very lovely things to look upon: a length of exquisite lace, an exotic Spanish-looking hair comb, a slim case of gold in which one might carry calling cards. Many treasures greeted her eye, but only one item truly caught her attention and held it.

Sara let loose her hold on Hugh's arm and stepped closer to the window, her gaze fixed upon a delicately painted ladies' fan. It was, she was sure, one of the least expensive items in the window, certainly not of the same caliber as some of the other costly merchandise alongside of which it was displayed; but the design on the fan was lovely and the painted colors were very much to her liking.

She didn't realize she had been staring at the little fan until she heard Hugh's voice beside her saying, "I see you have found something you can like, after all."

"It is lovely—one of the nicest things I have ever seen, in fact. But I didn't come to town to shop for trifles."

"No, being the excellent housekeeper that you are, you came solely for the purpose of engaging a household staff. But I don't think anyone may fault you if you were to take a short side-trip into one of the shops along the way." He added, in a most beguiling voice, "Of a certain, I shall never tell anyone."

Sara was clearly tempted. Dearly would she have loved to possess that little fan; how well it would look with her favorite evening gown! But when Mr. Deverill offered to escort her into the shop to inquire after the price of the coveted trinket, she realized in an instant that she dare not do so. She had, she knew, only a small amount of money in her possession left over from her last quarter-day allowance; she knew, too, that the meagerly clutch of bills in her reticule represented all the money left to put food on the table and run the household.

Under any other circumstance, Sara would have purchased the lovely little fan without a second thought, but she was no longer in a position to do so. Now, with Philip's gaming debts and the shabby state of Carvington Hall, it was left to Sara to be the sensible one; it was left to Sara to finance the household from the little money she had left.

If only Philip had not gambled away all their money, she might never have found herself in such a position; if only Philip had not fallen in with the likes of Hugh Deverill, she might have spent her own pin money freely and purchased the little fan. She did not begrudge helping her brother; she did, however, object to the fact that were it not for Hugh Deverill and his horrid influence, she and her brother might never have found themselves in their present straightened circumstances to begin with.

"Well?" Hugh murmured, quite close beside her. "Shall we go in?"

Sara turned to face him with much the same expression of denial Eve might have worn when first tempted by the serpent. "No, Mr. Deverill, we shall not! I think you forget my situation!"

He looked more amused than offended, and said beguilingly, "Never mind your situation. I know *I* certainly don't!" Hugh possessed himself of her small, gloved hand and tucked it again over his arm. In general, he was accounted something of an expert in the gentle art of seduction, and he had certainly known a sufficient amount of success in wrapping pretty housemaids around his little finger. So far, Miss Sara of Carvington Hall had proved to be a bit more resistant than most such domestic girls, but he didn't think she would be able to resist him for very much longer. He looked down at her, fairly well convinced that with a few more well-chosen compliments he would at last see the light of attraction in her eyes. But instead of looking up at him in admiration, she had about her a look of outrage. Clearly, she was angry. Just as Hugh formed the notion that it might prove amusing to discover what, if anything, was behind the latest change in her rather quick-silver emotions, he saw that her attention had been distracted by a gentleman on the street.

"Sara?" asked the man, in a tone of wonder, as he came upon them. "By Jove, it *is* you! Almost I didn't know you! What a beauty you have become! Here, let me take a look at you!"

Chapter Five

There was no mistaking the look of obvious pleasure in the gentleman's eyes when they lit upon Sara. Hugh, glancing in a disarmingly indifferent fashion toward Sara, caught the smile of greeting that graced her lips, as well.

Sara held out her hand to the gentleman and he immediately enveloped it between the warmth of his own two hands. "Lord Westbury!" she said, well pleased. "How do you do?"

"Very well! Very well, indeed!" he replied, in great enjoyment. His eyes settled appreciatively upon her and the smile he cast her was a measure of his fond regard. "So you are returned to us at last! Why, you were little more than a girl when you went away and now look at you! You are a delight!"

Sara found herself blushing at the unexpected comment. A handsome figure of a man, Lord Westbury had long been a friend of her father's. When her papa had died, his lordship had been a kind and steadying influence

for Sara and her brother. Always she had thought of him
as someone older, someone wise and stable. Now, as she
looked up at him and met his gaze, she thought she saw
a spark of admiration in his eyes as they rested upon her.

She withdrew her hand from his and said, still flushing,
"You are very kind! It *has* been some time since last we
met, has it not? We have all changed a little, I think. Tell
me, do you know Mr. Deverill?"

Lord Westbury did, indeed. In fact, he was so well
acquainted with Hugh that he had been wondering, since
first coming upon them, what on earth Sara meant by
associating with such a man. Had it not been for Sara's
naïve introduction, Lord Westbury could have very well
ignored Hugh Deverill, but now that he was forced to
acknowledge him, his expression underwent a subtle
change.

The smile that had so charmingly graced his lordship's
lips a moment before, though it remained, froze a little,
and his expression turned from one of distinct pleasure
to one of guarded politeness.

For his part, Hugh bowed slightly and wondered, behind
expressionless eyes, what next would occur in the interesting little pantomime being played out before him. That
Sara was well acquainted with Lord Westbury there could
be no doubt; that she spoke to him not at all as a housekeeper might a peer of the realm was equally clear. He
resigned himself to the knowledge that he would have to
be teased a little while longer before he could discover how
Sara might come to know such a man as Lord Westbury.

His lordship, at Sara's introduction, said a little cau-
tiously, "Everyone, I think, knows of Mr. Hugh Deverill.
We have met before once or twice."

Hugh looked upon him in bland amusement. "Oh, certainly more often than that! How else might you have
gained a reputation as my severest critic?"

"To be honest, Sara, our paths do not cross as frequently as Mr. Deverill may make it sound. I, you see, have no taste for gaming hells."

"While I rarely enter a church," interpolated Mr. Deverill.

There was something about this exchange that alarmed Sara no small degree and she acted to divert both gentlemen, saying, "Mr. Deverill was kind enough to drive me to town so I may perform some errands. I thanked him most thoroughly and did not mean to detain him, but he insisted upon accompanying me."

"In that situation, at least, he was correct," said Lord Westbury. "It would not be right for you to walk about Bath unescorted. I, myself, was just walking south on Milsom Street—if you are bound in my direction, we could walk together."

"Then you shall have no further need of my escort. Westbury, if you will give me your promise to see Sara safely back to Carvington Hall, I shall take my leave of you," said Hugh. He was still possessed of Sara's gloved hand on his arm, and he raised it briefly to his lips in salute. "It has, as always, been a pleasure to be in your company, Sara." He released her with a smile that was so charming, she had an almost overwhelming urge to call him back.

But Lord Westbury was already offering his arm in escort. He asked, most politely, "Shall we walk on? Only tell me where you are bound and I shall escort you the remainder of the way there."

"I was on my way to the domestic agency. I intend to hire some servants for Carvington Hall."

"That is an enormous task for a girl just out of school," said his lordship, impressed.

"It is, I'm afraid, rather daunting," confessed Sara, "but it is a task that must be done. Only, I don't know how I shall manage it, for I have no experience in this sort of thing.''

"Then you must allow me to help. Why do you look at me so? You doubt that my offer to assist you is sincere? I assure you, it is! I have quite a bit of experience in negotiating a fair price for a service rendered. Let me help you in this, Sara.''

His offer could not have come at a better time. With some relief she accepted, saying, "Thank you! I wasn't exactly sure how I should go about the business, but with you beside me, I am sure I shall do very well, indeed.''

"You may leave all to me. Now, will you allow me to offer you another piece of advice on another matter?''

"Of course!''

"I shall say this as delicately as I am able, but, Sara, it is not at all a good thing for you to be seen in the company of a man such as Hugh Deverill. My dear, I fear he is one gentleman who is not to be trusted.''

"Unnecessary to tell me, I assure you!'' she answered, promptly. "He is a friend of Philip's, though, and as long as he remains at Carvington Hall, I fear I must tolerate his company.''

Lord Westbury frowned. "Do you mean to tell me the man is living in the same house as you?''

"Yes, it's true. He and his friend, Lord Hetherington, are both guests in the house.''

Lord Westbury was silent for a moment, then he said, gravely, "I was under the impression that there was no one left at Carvington Hall but Philip.''

"There is Daisy, the maid. But aside from me there is no one in residence, if that is what you mean.''

"Under those circumstances, Philip should never have invited two gentlemen to stay. Sara, your remaining in a house full of bachelors is rather extraordinary.''

"Mr. Deverill is not a gentleman I wish to have as a guest

in our home for any longer than necessary," said Sara, with feeling. "Philip has assured me that Mr. Deverill shall leave within two day's time. He promised!"

"His departure cannot come too soon, I think," said his lordship darkly.

"How is it you come to know Mr. Deverill?" asked Sara. "You are so dissimilar, I am frankly surprised the two of you are acquainted."

"My mother was quite good friends with Deverill's mother at one time. They still exchange the odd letter every so often, I believe. His family, you know, is excellent, and the entire lot of them are as rich as Croesus. Hugh is the youngest of the Deverills of my generation and he is something of a bad egg, I'm afraid. His mother suffers tremendous heartache because of it, I am sure. His reputation is—forgive me! I shouldn't speak so. Let us just say his reputation is not fit to recommend him as a proper escort for a young lady such as you."

Sara digested this cryptic remark and asked, doubtfully, "Is—is he *very* bad?"

Lord Westbury smiled kindly. "I don't wish to distress you, but I cannot think him a suitable companion for you or your brother."

"I suspected as much. He has, I fear, a certain influence over Philip. I think my brother admires him a great deal and tries to emulate him."

"I see. Would it help at all if I were to speak to Philip?"

"If only you would, I should be very grateful!"

"Then I shall do so. You know, for some time now I have had a special interest in you and your brother. I know how difficult it has been, losing first your mother, then your father and being left to fend for yourselves. You may rely upon me, Sara, for anything you may need."

There was something infinitely comforting in the way he placed his fingers over her hand as it lay nestled in the crook of his arm. When Lord Westbury looked gently down upon her and smiled assuringly, Sara found that she was quite convinced that his lordship had only the best interests of her brother and herself at heart.

After being exposed to Mr. Deverill's somewhat rakish behavior and horrid influence over Philip, it was rather comforting to find herself in the presence of such a level-headed and virtuous man. Surely, she reasoned, Philip would be just as glad as she to renew his acquaintance with Lord Westbury. Then it would be merely a matter of time before her dear brother realized that his lordship was a much better pattern card and friend than wicked Mr. Deverill could ever hope to be.

Philip did not agree. When Sara chanced to tell him a little later that day that she had happened upon Lord Westbury in town and had spent the better part of the afternoon in his company, Philip was a little bit astounded.

He scowled at her and said, as if he were not quite sure he had understood her correctly, "And you conversed with Westbury? Right there in front of Deverill?"

"Why, yes," she answered, "and his lordship remarked that he was very pleased to see me again."

"Well, if ever a sister could be more of a knock-in-the-cradle!" he exclaimed in exasperation. "And while you were making conversation with Westbury like a grand dame of society, what was Deverill thinking, I should like to know?"

"I—I don't know," admitted Sara. "I suppose he was merely listening to what we were saying. How could he do otherwise?"

"Or perhaps he was wondering how a chit of a girl who is supposed to be nothing more than a housekeeper should come to be on such friendly terms with a peer of the realm? Eh? Did you ever consider that, I should like to know?"

Sara felt her cheeks color slightly. "Goodness, I didn't think of that!"

"Perhaps not, but I assure you, Deverill did!"

"No, I do not think he noticed anything out of the way," said Sara, after a bit of reflection. "At least, he didn't *seem* to behave as if he thought my conversation with Lord Westbury was at all odd."

"You may thank your lucky stars for that," he said, sounding a good deal relieved. "But merely because Deverill suspects nothing doesn't mean you may let your guard down, Sara. Dash it, if you mean to carry off this business and have him think you're the housekeeper, you shall have to behave like one!"

"But what am I to do when Lord Carville calls upon us?"

"Good lord, does he mean to?"

"Why, yes, Philip. I told you that he means to renew his acquaintance with us, and especially with you."

"God help us!" said Philip, dampeningly. "Well, if he does call, I shall merely say that you are out. You mustn't see him, do you understand? And Sara—in the future, I should take it very kindly if you would be a bit more careful what you are about when Deverill is in earshot."

Sara pursed her lips together and counted to ten before answering, with a hint of temper, "Philip Carville, I could cuff your ears! Of all the wretched things to say to me, when it was you who created this ghastly situation! It wasn't my wish to impress such a horrid man as Hugh Deverill, nor did I at all wish to suffer his cheeky behavior all the way into Bath!"

"Well, if you don't like the man, there's a very easy remedy you might adopt: you might stay away from him!"

"Believe me, I shall!" retorted Sara, her temper now in full reign. "Nothing should please me more than to stay far, far away from Mr. Hugh Deverill!"

Chapter Six

Sara wiped her hands on the full apron she wore and paused a moment from her labors to push a few stray strands of gold-brown hair back from her forehead. She had, she thought, good reason to feel very well pleased with what she saw as she surveyed the state of the hall. The walnut paneled walls had been dusted and buffed to a rich shine and the floors had been mopped and buffed as well. Every bit of brass had been polished and the banister that followed the graceful curve of the staircase as it wound its way to the upper stories had been waxed until she almost thought she could see her reflection in its surface.

Thanks to Lord Westbury's excellent negotiating skills, Sara's visit to the employment agency the day before had been fruitful, indeed. She had managed to engage the services of not only a cook, a footman and a housemaid, but a scullery girl, as well.

Immediately upon their arrival at Carvington Hall, the new servants had been put to work. Within hours Sara had begun to see a difference from their efforts; within a day she noticed that the hall was at last beginning to resemble the magnificent room of her memory. She proudly showed Philip the gleaming entry hall and she could tell he was dutifully impressed with her efforts.

"You're a wonder, Sara!" he exclaimed after inspecting one of the table tops and finding no trace of dust or finger smudges. "Why, the old hall hasn't looked so splendid in at least a year, I should say. Capital, that's what I call it— capital! Now, if you will only take the rest of the house in hand!"

She could not have been more pleased. "I intend to do just so, Philip. In fact, I plan to set the staff to work on the reception rooms today, as soon as your guests are gone."

"Gone? Oh, they're not leaving today. Didn't I tell you? Hetherington and Deverill have decided to stay on. Isn't that famous?"

"Infamous, more like!" exclaimed Sara, with a mixture of alarm and anger. "Philip, you promised they would be gone today! You promised!"

"Well, their plans have changed, that's all!" answered Philip, unable to understand the reason behind her sudden flash of anger. "I'm sure if they were *your* guests, you wouldn't wish them in Jericho!"

"If they were *my* guests, *you* wouldn't be made to act the part of a housekeeper! Philip, don't you see that they must be made to leave? How much longer must this charade continue?"

Philip made a face. *"What* charade?"

"The charade we embarked upon so you could impress those two men. Philip, they think I am your housekeeper!"

"Well, of course they do," said her brother, reasonably. "After all, that's what we want."

"No, that's what *you* want. *I* want to go to the assemblies and the theater and know everything the Bath season has to offer!"

"Well I ain't holding you back. Go to the blasted assemblies, if you like!"

Sara drew a deep breath for patience. "But, Philip, think! How are you to accompany me to a theater if I am thought to be merely the housekeeper?"

"Don't be daft!" he said, casting her a look of scorn. "I ain't going to the theater—with you or anyone else! Whatever put such a slummy notion in your head, I can't begin to think! Theater, indeed!"

For a moment, Sara was too stunned to speak; then she said, her temper in full career, "Of all the selfish, wretched things to say! How *could* you say such a thing, when I have done everything you have asked of me! I regret ever having agreed to this horrid scheme!"

"You may save your regret, Miss Sassy. In case you have forgotten why we embarked upon this little masquerade in the first place, may I remind you that all those precious trips to the assembly and the theater you keep talking about cost money, and we haven't two pennies to rub together. If ever I am to recover some of the money I sent Deverill's way, I need to court his good opinion. Without his countenance, we're lost, and that's a fact; so you may save yourself the trouble of looking at me as ugly as bull-beef and kindly remember that I'm doing this partially for you!"

"I don't need Hugh Deverill's money!" Sara retorted, still angry. "What's more I don't want it! I should rather live in poverty than on a thousand pounds from Hugh Deverill!"

"Nice! Very pretty indeed!" uttered Philip over his shoulder as he stomped off in anger.

Sara left the hall in the opposite direction, her rampant temper warring with an overwhelming need to cry. She threw open the first door she came to, seeking a place of quiet and privacy where she could give in to her tears of frustration.

She tumbled through the library door and was half-way across the room before she realized she was not alone and that Mr. Deverill and Lord Hetherington were there before her. Both gentlemen were on their feet in an instant but Sara was sure that her brimming eyes and trembling chin did not go unnoticed.

Hugh stepped forward. His hand stretched out to her, then just as quickly, fell to his side. "Sara? Come in, won't you?"

She was already backing toward the door, having discovered her error. "Oh, no! I should never have entered— had I only known you were here . . ."

"You are perfectly welcome to stay, if you like. I was just telling Hetherington here about our excursion yesterday into Bath and that we had run into an old and mutual acquaintance."

Lord Hetherington's eyes widened. *"You* have a mutual acquaintance? You and the *housekeeper*? How can that be?"

Sara found herself flushing as two pairs of eyes directed rather questioning glances her way. It had never occurred to her that her friendship with Lord Westbury would draw suspicion upon herself. At the time, Mr. Deverill hadn't appeared to noticed that her conversation with Lord Westbury was out of character for a housekeeper. Apparently, she was mistaken; beneath those bored and sleepy eyelids that sometimes almost covered Mr. Deverill's grey eyes, he had seen much more than she had given him credit for. Now, under the pressure of Lord Hetherington's confounded expression and Hugh Deverill's cool yet penetrating gaze, she could hardly think of any plausible explanation to offer.

Hugh came to her rescue, saying, "Sara, it appears,

knows Lord Westbury. I dare say you came to know him
because you were employed by him before coming to work
here at Carvington Hall.''

"Yes. Yes, that is it exactly," she said, wondering how
many more lies she would be forced to utter before her
masquerade was at last at an end.

"Westbury, you say?" asked Lord Hetherington. "And
you encountered him here in Bath? Oh, Lord, save us all!''

That exclamation was enough to rekindle a spark from
Sara's anger. "What, pray, do you mean, my lord?"

"I mean that the man is a cursed pattern card! Not a
one of us can hope to compare well to him!''

Unable to trust that she had correctly divined a note of
sarcasm in Lord Hetherington's tone, Sara looked from
his lordship to Hugh, then back again. "Are—are you well
acquainted with Lord Westbury?" she asked.

"Heavens, no! I make it a policy, in fact, to remain
as unacquainted with him as possible! The man has no
imagination, no flair! I consider him the dullest dog alive."

For the second time in less than five minutes, Sara felt
her temper rise to the fore. "I beg to differ with you, Lord
Hetherington! I find Lord Westbury to be far from dull! His
conversation is entertaining and his manners are beyond
criticism. He is helpful and intelligent and a man I would
wish might have a greater influence over—" She stopped
short, realizing that she had verged on a gross indiscretion.
She had almost wished that Lord Westbury might have a
greater influence over Philip. No mere housekeeper would
be forgiven uttering such things to men like Mr. Deverill
and Lord Hetherington and she could only hope she had
stopped herself in time.

"My dear young woman," said Lord Hetherington in a
frigid voice as he looked down upon her through his quizzing glass, "I accede that Westbury is everything you have
said; he is, indeed, a man of excellent character. Perhaps

that is the reason I would not wish to find myself in his company for any length of time."

It was all Sara could do to bite her tongue and hold back the words she would most like to have hurled in Lord Hetherington's direction. Her departure from the library was abrupt; her dislike of the men she left behind there, intense.

She was still smarting some time later from the injustice of Lord Hetherington's criticisms and the unfairness of her own situation when she chanced upon Philip on the second floor landing.

He was dressed to go out for the evening, and looked the very picture of a young gentleman of fashion. "There you are, Sara. I went looking for you all afternoon. Where have you been hiding yourself?"

She shook her head. "Nowhere in particular. I merely wished to be alone from a while."

"A bit tired, are you, of having a house full of men?" he asked, sympathetically. "Well, you'll have all the time you need for solitude tonight. I'm off for Bath with Hetherington and Deverill for the evening. I've even got myself a new waistcoat for the occasion. Tell me, what do you think of it?" He held open the lapels of his coat, the better for Sara to inspect his newest piece of finery. "Do you like it?"

"A new waistcoat? But, why, Philip? Why did you buy it?"

"I had to have something to wear tonight. I've been seen too often already in my yellow brocade and my blue waistcoat has got a stain."

"Yes, but, Philip, this one looks very expensive. Did it not cost you quite a bit?"

"It didn't cost me anything, for I bought it on tick," said Philip, happily.

Sara was too astonished by this bit of logic to answer

straight away. After a moment she said, with infinite patience, "But, Philip, merely because you buy something on credit does not mean the item is free."

"I know that! I simply meant to say that I didn't have to lay my lolly down on the spot. It was Deverill's doing, really. He had merely to take me to his tailor and say the word, and—lo, and behold!—I was the owner of a new waistcoat purchased on credit."

"Mr. Deverill!" she uttered, her face flushing with sudden anger. "I should have known his horrid influence would figure somehow!"

"Here, now, what do you mean by that?" demanded Philip.

A deep feeling of resentment welled up within her. She ignored his question, saying instead, "Philip, how could you buy a new waistcoat for yourself? How could you allow Mr. Deverill to talk you into making a purchase that we can ill afford?"

"I've already told you, it cost me nothing. Why, I won't even see the reckoning for it until after I've received my next quarter-day allowance. Why are you so angry?"

"Because you are dressed in new finery while I am being made to wear mourning clothes that were new the year our mother died," she retorted. "And I'm angry because I am the one who is making all the sacrifices while you are enjoying all the benefits of the bargain we struck."

"Well, that simply ain't true!" protested Philip, in weak defense. "I'm making sacrifices, as well, you know! I'm the one that must figure a way out of our predicament and replenish our coffers!"

"Do you mean the coffers you helped drain in the first place?" demanded Sara.

"I can see there's no point talking to you when you get in such a mood!" said Philip, furiously. In high dudgeon he started down the stair, saying, "I can only hope you shall have regained your good nature by the time I return!"

"Where are you going?"

He paused and turned back. "I'm going into Bath with Deverill and Hetherington."

A faint reminder of her earlier tears welled up in Sara's eyes. "What will you do in Bath?"

With a rare perception, Philip noticed the change in his sister's expression. He saw the moisture of unshed tears glimmering in the light of the candles in the hallway and he saw, too, the troubled look in her eyes. His anger melted quickly away and he said, very gently, "We shall do this and that, I suppose. If we can find a card game, we shall be well pleased. If not, we shall just have to find some other entertainments."

"But, Philip, don't you understand? *I* want to attend the entertainments in Bath, too," she said, wistfully.

"Well, lud, don't I know that, Sara? Now, let's not stir up this afternoon's coals, eh? Don't think I don't know how much help you've been to me and what a good sister you are. Why, you're as good as ever twanged, I should think, but—" He stopped short, his attention arrested by the sound of a few notes played on the pianoforte in the drawing room downstairs. "Why, that must be Hetherington plunking those keys. He told me once he played, you know, but I've never heard him do so."

"Philip," said Sara, determined to draw his attention back to the matter at hand, "please reconsider taking me to one of the assemblies in town. Please?"

"I'll tell you what—as soon as Deverill and Hetherington are gone, we shall speak of this. Upon my honor, we shall! But right now, I must join Hetherington in the library. He's probably wondering what the deuce is keeping me away, as it is!" Philip exclaimed, and he went quickly down the stairs.

His words left Sara feeling far from comforted; indeed, she felt her anger rise again. She wished most heartily she were as free as Philip that she might attend any number of the assemblies, parties, or theater performances in Bath.

For a few moments she remained on the stair landing, listening to the music from the pianoforte meander in random notes of no particular order. After a little while, she heard the music stop. When it resumed, Sara listened to one of the prettiest tunes she had heard in some time. It was a lovely piece, one that reminded Sara of all the assemblies and the dancing she was missing in town; each note reminded her of the opera performances she would not be present to see.

Still, the music was beautiful and, wishing to hear it clearly, she made her way to the long gallery. An expansive room with high ceilings and polished floors, the gallery was situated directly above the drawing room. Clearly could she hear the music from the pianoforte and she was reminded of the balls her mother and father had hosted when she was a little girl. Their guests had danced in that very room, and Sara longed to be able to do the same.

But no amount of wishing could bring Sara a dance partner to whisk her down the length of the gallery, nor could a wish send her to one of the balls or assemblies in town. Rather dismally she resigned herself to the fact that, for tonight, at least, she would have to be content to listen to the music from the pianoforte.

In the drawing room, Philip watched as Lord Hetherington stopped playing a rather lovely waltz on the pianoforte in favor of banging out a few chords of music on the keys.

Philip himself was an indifferent musician, but he thought he recognized the piece his lordship was attempting to play and, if memory served him, it was being played very ill, indeed.

He said, "I should think Deverill will be along any moment and we can leave for town. I wonder that he isn't down here already."

"He'll be along," said Lord Hetherington, loud enough to be heard over the sounds of the pianoforte.

Philip listened a minute or two longer. "I didn't know you played, Hetherington."

His lordship stopped playing and turned slightly in his chair, the better to see Philip. "I fill my life with beauty, dear boy. All the accomplishments are mine! I see by your expression that you doubt me! You don't truly believe I am master of this instrument, do you? You wrong me, dear boy; you wrong me!" And so saying, Lord Hetherington turned back to the pianoforte and began to play a waltz that was quite the loveliest sound Philip had ever heard. No fitful starts and stops marred his performance; he played the waltz perfectly and with all the feeling of a concert performer.

Upstairs in the long gallery, Sara was just as impressed as Philip by what she heard. The music of the pianoforte came up from the drawing room below in mellow, rich tones and Sara found herself responding to it. Almost without even being aware, Sara's feet began to move in time across the floor of the gallery. How dearly would she have loved to be moving thus at an assembly in town, but if that wish was not meant to come true, at least she could enjoy the music now.

She lifted her skirts in one hand and dipped a curtsy to an imaginary partner. With an innate grace and a care-lessness she had not felt since her return home, Sara began to move in rhythm about the room. Easy indeed was it for her to lose herself in her dance; the music was beautifully played and so rapt was she in wonder of the moment, that she quite gave herself up to the enjoyment of her dance.

Time lost its relevance, inhibitions were cast to the winds; Sara turned and swayed to the music, oblivious to anything else, until a daring pirouette, executed in the passion of the moment, brought her face to face with Hugh Deverill.

Chapter Seven

Hugh was standing in the doorway to the gallery, watching Sara, his back straight and his face void of any expression. How long he had stood thus, she did not know, but surely he had been there long enough to have divined her actions.

Sara gave a sharp gasp and her cheeks immediately gained two telltale spots of color. She should have asked him what he meant by such behavior; she should have demanded that he leave at once. But she found, instead, that her embarrassment was so acute, her surprise at seeing him was so overwhelming, she could not utter a word. She merely stood, rooted to the spot, wondering in a rather crazed fashion what he meant to do next.

He showed her. Without a word Hugh traversed the distance between them and with every step he took, Sara's heart beat a little bit faster. When he was at last standing before her, standing so close she could reach out and touch him, he, instead, touched her. One of his strong hands snaked about her waist and the other clasped her hand in a light but compelling grip. Still silent, his grey eyes locked in a gaze with her blue ones, he took a step. Sara followed. Before she could even realize what they were about she found that she was dancing with Hugh Deverill down the length of the gallery.

She never tried to resist; indeed, Sara found she could only stare up at him, conscious only of his arm about her waist, of her small hand enveloped in the warmth of his own. At school Sara had taken lessons in dance, but no amount of tutelage could have prepared her for the sensation of being held in a man's arms. She felt as if she had suffered a small electric shock and her breath came to her in small little wisps.

Again and again they circled the room, and Hugh's arm tightened about her, drawing her closer to him, his gaze never wavering from her face.

From the drawing room, the music came to a stop and with it, their dance ended but Hugh didn't release her immediately. He stood a moment. At last he stepped away a bit and, still without uttering a word, he bent over her hand and brought it tenderly to his lips.

She was sure he heard her gasp; heaven knew she was having a difficult time drawing a full and steadying breath. But just as she thought he might take her in his arms once again, just when she hoped he would whirl her again about the floor with the same grace and enchantment he had only moments before, Hugh released her entirely.

With purposeful strides he made his way down the length of the long room toward the door. In an instant he was gone, leaving Sara alone and believing almost that she had just emerged from a dream.

But she had not dreamed it; for she knew very well that Hugh Deverill had held her as tenderly, as lovingly as she had ever been held in her life, and she knew a strong desire that he should do so again.

It was a difficult thing indeed for Sara to realize that she could find herself so attracted to the very man whose principles she held in strict aversion. He was the instrument of her brother's ruin, the impetus behind Philip's slide into dun territory. Yet there was now no denying that she was strongly and foolishly drawn to him. It was beyond all reason, and the realization robbed her of several precious hours of sleep that night, and continued to trouble her well into the next morning.

Sara did not see Hugh at breakfast, nor did she encounter him in any of the reception rooms of the house. While she would have been terribly embarrassed to have done so, she could not help feeling a trifle disappointed. She enlisted Daisy's escort on her walk into town to execute a number of errands, and still so rapt was she in her own thoughts of Hugh Deverill, that she was barely aware of Daisy's attempts to engage her in idle conversation. At last, receiving no response to any of her questions or observations, Daisy abandoned all attempts to engage her mistress in conversation and they completed their walk to town in silence.

Even while walking through the streets of Bath, Sara's thoughts remained on Hugh. She executed her errands as if she were moving through the fog of a curious dream. When the course of one of her errands caused her to pass the little shop where she and Hugh had paused two days before, she couldn't help but stop and stare wistfully at the little painted fan in the shop window.

She might have stood there for some time, with Daisy in curious silence beside her, had not Lord Westbury again come upon her much as he had earlier that week.

He interrupted her reverie, saying, "Sara, I am in luck again! Only good fortune could be thanked for causing our paths to cross twice in two days! Tell me, where are you bound? I have an appointment on Russell Street and will be happy to walk with you, if you are traveling in the same direction."

"I am well, thank you," she answered, smiling, "but I am bound in the opposite direction."

"On your way to the Pump Room, are you?"

"No. No, I am merely in town to accomplish a few errands—nothing could be less entertaining, I assure you!"

"Then we shall see what we can do to change that! I have a box at the opera, you know, and I'm escorting my mother there tomorrow night. Say you will come! Say you and Philip will join us and make a party of it."

No words he might have uttered could have lifted Sara's spirits more. "My lord! What a delightful invitation!"

"I'm glad I could please you," he said, watching her reaction with a growing warmth in his eyes. "I shall count on you tomorrow. And Philip," he added, as an afterthought. "Don't fail, now. Our box is large and there is room for everyone. Say you will come!"

"Of course!" she answered promptly. "We shall be delighted to accept your invitation."

Lord Westbury shook her hand and went on his way and Sara, feeling much more lighthearted, resumed her walk in the opposite direction.

Having witnessed Sara's conversation with Lord Westbury, Daisy walked beside her mistress in silence for a moment or two. Then, as if she could no longer contain herself, she exclaimed, with enthusiasm, "I should think the handsomest men in England are here in Bath!"

Sara laughed slightly. "Now, what on earth could make you say so?"

"Certainly, his lordship is as fine as wax. He's just the sort of gentleman a girl does dream about, I think. If that stick pin in the folds of his cravat were any indication, I do believe his pockets are warm and full." She looked expectantly up at Sara, awaiting her response. No such response was offered, and Daisy said, helpfully, "He'd make a fine husband, if a young lady was to wish it."

"Now, Daisy," Sara said in a warning tone, "I would appreciate your not marrying me off quite yet, if you don't mind."

"I shouldn't want to do that, miss, for how, indeed, would you be able to make up your mind and choose between them? There's his lordship, of course, and it would be nice as cream to marry him and have a title, I should think. But if you were to fancy a truly handsome man, you must needs choose one of the London gentlemen."

"One of Philip's friends? You mean Lord Hetherington or Mr. Deverill? You're talking nonsense! Whatever put the notion in your head that I would consider marrying either one of them?"

"Well, miss, they are very handsome men," offered Daisy, as if that alone were enough to recommend them.

"Daisy, you cannot judge a man merely by the way he looks. Only think of Mr. Deverill as an example: he may be quite handsome, as you say, but that doesn't mean he is worthy of one's trust."

Her maid looked at her in astonishment. "With eyes like his?"

"There you go again, Daisy, willing to judge a person based upon their form or figure! I, on the other hand, cannot countenance forming an attachment for a man merely because he has beautiful eyes."

"Well, *I* never said Mr. Deverill's eyes were beautiful, now did I? I merely meant that his eyes do have a way of watching you, I've noticed. When you're in a room together, his eyes follow you wherever you move, that's all."

A faint flush covered Sara's cheeks and she tried to cover her discomfort by saying, carelessly, "I'm sure you're imagining such things!"

"Perhaps, but it did cross my mind, miss, that Mr. Deverill might be a bit smitten with you and that's what made me think you might be in the way of choosing him for a husband."

Sara tried to mask her blush with a tone of unconcern. "Believe me, Daisy, you have everything wrong! Mr. Deverill is hardly the kind of man who would ever consider marrying. Even if he were, I am not at all the sort of female who would tempt him toward the altar."

They arrived at the next shop on their list of establishments that must be visited and while Sara executed her errand there, Daisy held her tongue. As soon as they were back out on the walkway in front of the shop, she said, with all sincerity, "Me mum liked to say that a man won't keep a cow when he may have a quart of milk for a penny."

Startled, Sara stopped walking and demanded, in a voice of deep astonishment, "Your mother said, *what?*"

"A man won't keep a cow when he may have a quart of milk for a penny," recited Daisy. "That's what me mum used to tell me about men. She'd say, 'Now, Daisy, you be a good girl and do right with a gentleman, and he'll do right by you.' "

Sara shook her head and bit back an impulse to laugh. "I'm sure I don't know what you mean. Daisy, what on earth are you talking about?"

"I'm talking about Mr. Deverill, of course, and what you said about him and marriage. Don't you see, miss? Mr. Deverill is just like me mum said: he doesn't need to own a cow. Why should he when he can have all the benefits of a cow for so little expense and trouble on his part? That's how it's been, I figure. All his life, he's had his pick of women, and some very fine women, I'm sure. But one day he'll meet a very nice young lady, like yourself, who wants to do right, and, just like a cow, he won't be able to get any milk from her—if you know what I mean!—and he'll have to think about marrying her."

"That's the most astonishing analogy I've ever heard," said Sara, in a tone of wonder.

"But you have to admit, it do make sense."

"To a milkmaid, perhaps! But I am not a milkmaid, nor am I a cow, Daisy."

"No, miss, you're not, but that's not my point!"

"What *is* your point?"

"My point is, a gentleman may kiss a woman and make up to a woman, but that doesn't mean he'll marry the woman. All I'm saying is that it's ladies like you, who are good and who hold a man off a bit that they end up marrying. At least, that's what me mum told me, and me mum was always right!"

"Forgive me for disagreeing, but your mother could not have been thinking of Mr. Deverill when she gave you such advice!" said Sara, laughingly. "I think even your mother would find that Mr. Deverill is the exception to every rule!"

She was still laughing softly when she turned to resume her walk down the street. She hadn't ventured many steps when she spied Mr. Deverill driving his curricle up the street with a decided flair. He spied her and pulled up immediately, sending Jim Cotton to his horses' heads.

He touched his gloved hand to the brim of his hat and said, "Sara! Shopping, I see. Tell me, how many more stops have you to make?"

Keenly conscious of the fact that she had just finished making Mr. Deverill the subject of her conversation with Daisy, Sara found herself blushing somewhat. "I have finished, I think. I was just about to begin our walk home."

"Then let me drive you."

She took a step back. ''I wouldn't wish to interrupt your drive.''

''You won't. Jim will see the maid back and I shall promise to be on my best behavior. Come!'' He held out his hand to her expectantly.

''Very well, but only because you have promised!'' she said, taking his hand and allowing him to draw her up onto the seat beside him.

''Stand away, Jim!'' he said to his groom as he set the curricle in motion. ''I shall see you presently at the Hall.''

For the first few minutes of their drive, Hugh was obliged to concentrate on the traffic of the town roads but as soon as he had negotiated the turn onto Belmont Street and they were past Montpelier Road, he was able to relax a bit and direct a certain amount of attention toward Sara.

''If I drive too fast, you must, of course, tell me.''

''Not at all,'' she said, happily feeling the breeze rustle her curls. ''I quite enjoy a brisk drive, although it will blow my bonnet about!''

He studied her a moment. ''I think I liked better the bonnet you wore the last time I found you in my curricle. It had those blue ribbons on it and they matched your eyes quite fetchingly.''

Sara drew a deep breath for patience. ''I thought you promised to be on your best behavior!''

''Paying compliments *is* my best behavior,'' he said, smiling. ''Would you rather I spoke of the weather?''

''Yes!''

''A woman who does not wish to be paid compliments— you're an unusual young woman.''

''I am merely a housekeeper,'' she said, in a prim tone she hoped would discourage him.

''Yes, so you keep telling me.'' After that he fell to silence and Sara was able to let her guard down enough to enjoy the drive and the passing countryside. They approached the intersection where the Road to Gloucester commenced, the very road that would take them back to Carvington Hall. As they neared the intersection, Hugh swung his horses to the left, up Lansdown Place.

"But this is not the way!" exclaimed Sara. "You should have remained on the Gloucester Road!"

"I know. Tell me, when was the last time you drove to Lansdown Hill? I assure you, it is a much more pleasant drive since the roads were improved."

"But you said you would drive me to Carvington Hall," she protested, weakly.

"And so I shall," he answered with a slight smile. "But first, let me prove to you that I can be a man of pleasant company when I wish to be."

She flushed, feeling as if he was very well aware of her opinion of him. "I—I never thought otherwise!"

"Yes, you did, but no matter—I never took it to heart!"

It was clear to Sara that he was intent upon teasing her, no matter what she might say. She turned her head away, determined to ignore him and she became interested again in the scenery.

Mr. Deverill's horses drew the light curricle up the hill with ease; they passed several other carriages, and some pedestrians, too, all making their way up or down the hill. They reached the top of the rise and found a clutch of vehicles assembled at the crest, their occupants intent upon the excellent view of the cities of Bath and Bristol.

Hugh drew the curricle to a stop and they sat for a while in companionable silence, looking down from their vantage point at the Bristol Channel and the ships at harbor. "Well?" he asked, after a while.

"It's quite lovely. I had no idea one could see so far from these hills. Thank you for bringing me!"

"This is one of my favorite drives whenever I come to Bath. Unfortunately, it is also the favorite of too many others, I think. Driving up Lansdown Hill has become something of a fashionable thing to do in recent years."

Sara looked over to where a number of vehicles were pulled up together in a throng. "Those people look very fashionable, indeed. I have never seen such splendid carriages. There are so many of them, they are almost blocking the road."

One such carriage, an open landaulette with a single occupant, broke away from the group and headed toward their curricle and the road beyond that lead down the hill. No sooner did the carriage pull alongside them, than it drew to a halt. In it, a woman looked over at Hugh and smiled. She was, to Sara's eye, quite beautiful and she wore a driving pelisse of exquisite workmanship. Her bonnet sported a fashionable high crown and a dashing little plume, and she had in her gloved hand a dainty sunshade that she had been about to unfurl. She abandoned that plan in favor of reaching out her hand to Hugh and saying, with obvious pleasure, "My dear, Hugh! I did not know you were in Bath this time of year!"

"Nor I, you," he responded. "Forgive me for not climbing down to greet you, but I left my groom in town and there is no one to hold the horses. You are looking well, as always."

Her full lips parted in a pleasing smile and her grey eyes, peeping out from beneath the lace cap beneath her bonnet, shone happily. "As are you! It has been too long since last I saw you. Tell me, what has kept you away: horses or ladies?"

"Have you no shame?" he asked, his expression alert.

"None at all. Neither have you or you would have introduced me by now to your companion." The woman cast a questioning glance at Sara, who was suddenly not at all sure that she wanted to make the acquaintance of one of

Hugh Deverill's flirts, even one as lovely as this lady appeared to be.

"I beg your pardon," said Hugh. "Of course, let me make you known to each other. Sara is—Let us say she is staying at the house where I myself am a guest."

"Indeed?" asked the woman, her finely arched brows flying skyward. "How very cozy. What home might that be?"

"I am from Carvington Hall," said Sara, finding her voice at last.

"An excellent place, if I recall. I chanced to visit there many years ago, while traveling to Bristol with Lady West-bury, I think. Yes, an excellent place, Carvington Hall." She turned her attention back to Hugh. "I have put up at the White Hart in Bath. If you can find a moment to spare between card parties and visits to your gentleman's haunts, you'll visit me there, I hope!"

"It shall be my pleasure," said Hugh.

"Then I shall rely upon it." She signaled then to her coachman and her vehicle moved off, making its way slowly down the hill.

Hugh watched her progress a moment before he turned back toward Sara. "I hope I didn't make you uncomfortable just now, but I wasn't at all certain how I should introduce you."

"Why did you not introduce me as the subject of your latest pursuit?" she asked daringly, and found that, far from repulsed, he was instead rather amused. She decided to take advantage of his good humor and asked, "Tell me, who was that woman?"

He looked down at her, one brow cocked questioningly. "Did you like her?"

"Yes, I think I did. She is certainly beautiful and she is obviously smitten with you."

"I like to think so," he said, mildly.

"Have you—have you known her for very long?"

"All my life."

"Is she one of your flirts?"

"Yes, she is and I rather like her the best of all of them. You see, the lady you just met was my mother."

Sara looked up at him, astonished. "No! I don't think I can believe—" She stopped short, realizing that the same grey eyes into which she was looking at that very moment matched quite nicely the grey eyes that had belonged to the woman in the carriage. A further examination of his handsome face convinced Sara that they also shared the same line of their brow and the same strong, rather square chin. "You *are* telling the truth!" she said at last, in a voice of wonder.

"I have been known to tell the truth from time to time," he said, amiably as he set about turning his horses on the road.

"But you didn't tell me—I had no notion—oh, what must she think of me?"

He looked down in time to see her blushes rise above her collar and he smiled slightly. "She must only think, as I do, that you are quite the most charming young woman I have ever known."

Chapter Eight

Sara, in a state of rare anger, paced up and down the drawing room. She directed a fiery glance toward her brother. "Of all the odious, selfish, unfeeling creatures! Philip Brandon-Howe, I am quite displeased!"

"Stubble it," recommended Philip. "I ain't going to the theater! There!"

"But Lord Westbury's invitation was to both of us! If you do not go, I cannot possibly go! Please, Philip? Please do this for me, when I have been so obliging with your requests, no matter how inconvenient or distasteful they may be!"

Philip relented slightly and said in a more coaxing tone than he had used thus far, "Now don't cut up rough on me, Sara. Truly, I shouldn't mind dangling you from my arm another time, but tonight Deverill has lined up a very tight little card party in town. How, I should like to know, am I to attend it if I am squiring you about the theater?"

"Oh, Philip, please don't go gambling tonight!"

"I have to," he said, moving uneasily about the drawing room. "I need to win some money, Sara, for I haven't two beans to rub together."

"But we shall receive next quarter's income in only one week's time. Then you shall have plenty of money—why, I shall give you some of mine, if you wish it."

He shook his head. "I need the fancy *now*. But what I don't need is you prosing at me like a Methodist."

"But, Philip—"

"I cannot miss this card party tonight, so don't ask it of me!"

Sara would have liked to have argued more, but there was something in her brother's demeanor that was a little desperate, a little bit as if he had suffered a most stunning blow, that caused her to refrain. The lines of strain about his eyes were more pronounced than before and Sara realized that it had been some time since last she had seen her brother smile.

Still, she could not hide the note of bitter disappointment in her voice as she said, "I shall send word to Lord Westbury that we must decline his invitation. But, Philip, I should dearly love to go to the theater tonight, more than anything in the world!"

"The theater?" repeated Hugh Deverill, entering the room with Lord Hetherington at his side. "I understand Bath offers a most excellent theater troupe and a talented opera company. Why, I wonder, have we never attended before, Hetherington?"

Philip looked at him in some astonishment. "Do—do you mean you would actually go?"

"Of course! Do I not attend the theater when in London? Apply to Hetherington here, if you doubt me."

" 'Tis true," said Lord Hetherington, most promptly. "Deverill will often attend theater parties, as will I. Why do you look at me with such surprise? I assure you, I have an artistic vein that runs quite deep!''

Hugh watched Sara's reaction. ''Then shall we make a party of it? Shall the four of us accept Westbury's invitation?''

Philip frowned slightly. ''But, but there's a card party tonight—it's one of the doings that dictated your coming to Bath in the first place.''

''Dictate?'' repeated Hugh, with a such a sharp look toward Philip that any further argument was effectively quelled. ''No one dictates my behavior, Carville. No one.''

''I didn't mean—of course, no one should dream of dictating to *you*, Deverill! I merely thought—Well, of course, if you wish to go, well, there can be no argument, can there?''

But Hugh thought he had plenty to argue over. In the brief moments in which he had stood poised in the doorway, before either Philip or Sara had noticed his presence, he had been provided an opportunity to observe them together and was instantly disturbed by what he saw there.

At first he thought he was mistaken, that some trick in the shadows cast by a late afternoon sun had fooled his eyes, making them untrustworthy. But just as quickly did he realize that there was nothing at all wrong with his vision. He would have been a sap-skull not to have seen how alike Philip's blue eyes were to Sara's, and how closely did the line of his jaw follow the same delicate course that framed Sara's lovely face. There was, he knew, no denying that there was a strong resemblance between them and he would have bet his last groat that they were brother and sister. They certainly argued as any brother and sister would and Hugh wondered why he had never realized their connection before.

Since the moment of his acquaintance with Sara, he had been presented with ample evidence that she was not as she claimed to be. She was too young, too pretty, to be a mere servant and he had long been of the opinion that neither her manner nor mien was that of a housekeeper.

What the devil she meant by posing as a mere servant, he could not guess; that her ruse was probably instigated by Philip, he had no doubt. If he knew anything of Carville's character—and he fancied he knew quite a bit, thank you very much—Carville had probably held Sara up at sword point to perform a part in such a ridiculous masquerade. Of a sudden he thought of all the times she had been forced to behave as a servant in her own house; how she had been made to wear day after day the same grey frocks when he was sure she had many more attractive gowns in her wardrobe; how she had stayed at home as any other servant would, instead of taking her place beside her peers in Bath society.

He wasn't sure what game Carville and his sister were playing, but he was suddenly seized with a keen determination to find out. He said, his voice and countenance quite impassive, "I should be disappointed if we did not avail ourselves of Westbury's invitation." He directed a look of bland inquiry toward Sara. "I assume his invitation was extended to Carville's guests, as well?"

His question threw her a little off balance. She had expected the same resistance from Hugh Deverill that she had been forced to weather from Philip. To find that Hugh was willing to forsake an opportunity to gamble in favor of attending an evening at the opera left her confused and a trifle suspicious.

"Do—do you mean you would go? You would attend the opera tonight instead of your card party?"

"It shall be my pleasure," he said, with perfect politeness.

There was no mistaking the small spark of happiness that suddenly light Sara's face. "Are—are you quite sure?"

she asked, fearful that she might have misinterpreted his words.

"I assure you, I have never been more certain of anything in my life."

She smiled then, a great, dazzling smile that, had he been a more sentimental fellow, might have warmed Hugh to his very soul.

"Then I must make sure I have something suitable to wear for the occasion," she said earnestly as she moved toward the door. "And my hair! I shall have to make it up into some very stylish arrangement and—oh, I have much to do before this evening. Please excuse me!"

Philip stared after her for a moment, quite confounded. "Well, if that doesn't beat anything!" he said, at last. "The theater for a gambling party! Next she'll have us attending temperance meetings and reading sermons from Hannah More! Dash it, Deverill, I—I don't know how this happened, truly I don't! But I assure you, I shall do my best to make her see sense!"

Hugh cast him a sidelong glance. "Leave things as they are, Carville. Don't tamper with her happiness."

"Yes, but—but the *opera!*" Philip exclaimed, as he opened the door and began to make his way toward the stairs. "I cannot fathom what you are thinking of, but I suppose if you say we shall see a performance tonight, then I have no choice but to go!"

Lord Hetherington closed the door upon him, saying, "Yes, yes, we'll all go! And won't Westbury be surprised to find us there!" Left at last alone with Hugh, his lordship cast him a pointed look. "Although I doubt Westbury could be half as surprised by our attendance as I am. I say, Deverill, whatever possessed you to put your elbow in my ribs when we walked in the room, just now?"

Hugh crossed to a small side table on which reposed a decanter and several glasses. He poured a glass of wine for Lord Hetherington, saying, "It was clumsy of me, I know, but I wanted you to follow my lead. You did, of course, and you said exactly what I wanted you to say."

"Then perhaps you would be good enough to tell me why we are going to the theater tonight instead of bleeding innocents at Black Jack Hardy's gambling party!"

Hugh poured out a glass for himself and took a thoughtful drink. "Because she wished it."

His lordship frowned. *"She?* Do you mean, the housekeeper?"

"She's no housekeeper," said Hugh, quietly, his brow furrowed in concentration.

"I shouldn't care if she were the queen herself! Listen here, Deverill! We've waited weeks for a chance to play cards with Hardy and now, at the latest possible moment, when the deck is at last about to be dealt, you change your mind! What the devil do you mean by it, eh?"

Hugh looked at him a moment, debating the wisdom of confiding to his friend his suspicions concerning Sara and her true status in the household. He decided against it and his eyes fell to the glass he held in his hand. He took another sip from it. "I mean to attend the opera, nothing more. You may join us, of course, or you may go to Hardy, it makes no difference to me."

Lord Hetherington cast him a look of dark suspicion. "What, exactly, are you up to, Deverill? What card have you got hidden in your sleeve, ready to produce at the very instant you need it most?"

"You wrong me, Hetherington. I never resort to such measures, I assure you. Must I have some ulterior motive merely because I prefer to spend my evening at the theater rather than in a darkened room with a deck of cards?"

"No, but—but tonight, of all nights! And with Westbury, of all people! I fear the entire evening shall be as dull as a doorknob!"

"On the contrary," said Hugh. "I have a feeling we shall find the evening to be vastly entertaining!"

"You'll excuse me, I know, if I disagree," said his lordship. "I'm not about to fob Hardy off now so don't ask it of me."

"I won't," said Hugh, simply.

"Then you don't object if I prefer to go to Hardy's gaming night instead of the opera with you?"

"Not at all. You must, of course, suit yourself. Make my apologies to Hardy, won't you?"

Lord Hetherington regarded him searchingly for a moment, his smooth brow puckered in concentration, and his eyes narrowed in slight suspicion. "What's got into you, Deverill?" he asked again. "What are you up to?"

Hugh refilled his glass, saying, "I cannot pretend to understand your meaning."

"I mean to say that this is not at all your usual behavior. You're acting strangely and I can tell you're up to something. Why, you look as though you've eaten a horse; yet you stand there, at your ease, trying to convince me that it's perfectly natural to see a tail hanging out of your mouth."

"I think you exaggerate, Jasper," said Hugh, one brow cocked in gentle amusement.

It was abundantly clear to his lordship that his greatest and closest friend was not about to confide the reason behind his extraordinary behavior. He issued one final plea to Hugh, begging him to reconsider and give up his plan to join Lord Westbury's opera party. But when Hugh declined yet again, Hetherington gave up and left the drawing room.

Hugh was rather glad of it, for he was aware of a growing flicker of annoyance that Lord Hetherington should continue to question his motives. In truth, he didn't know himself why he had changed his plans for the evening. Certainly, the card party he had so readily cast to the winds was the very reason he had ventured to Bath in the first place, but no sooner had he stood in the doorway of the drawing room and realized that Sara and Philip were brother and sister, than he was seized with an unaccustomed uncertainty.

In that instant of recognition had Hugh recalled all the little hints he had noticed but discounted concerning Sara. Her manner of dress, her elegant deportment, her contrary schoolgirl blushes; it had never occurred to him that she was the daughter of the house and he cursed himself that he hadn't seen it earlier.

No wonder he had thought her on such intimate terms with Carville! Little wonder, too, that she had behaved with such comfort with Westbury! She must have known the man since her days in cradle clothes! When he thought back to all the times he had attempted to flirt with her, only to have her respond so artlessly, he could have kicked himself.

But he became even more angry with himself when he chanced to recall that he had resolved to seduce her merely to while away a few pleasant hours. As a matter of honor, he was not in the habit of making love to schoolgirls and when he considered what the consequences might have been had he pursued that resolve to any stronger degree, he realized just how infamous his behavior had been.

He had misjudged her and he was angry with himself and a little ashamed for having done so. Upon further reflection, he found himself questioning what on earth might have occurred to have caused her to embark upon such a mad masquerade in the first place. He was certain it was Philip's idea; he was equally certain that Sara regretted agreeing to the scheme.

He had seen evidence of that regret in her eyes when he had come across Sara and Philip in the drawing room, and had overheard her pleas to go to the opera. His own reaction had surprised him, for truly, Hugh had not meant to forego his own entertainment in favor of pleasing a schoolgirl who was willing to dance whatever jig her foolish brother piped.

No sooner had he realized that she was Philip's sister than he realized, too, that she was trapped in an intolerable situation. Philip would never, he knew, free her from the deception he had designed. It was left then, to Hugh to find a way to end Sara's misguided masquerade. He wasn't yet certain how he was to accomplish the thing, but accomplish it, he would.

Chapter Nine

Hugh did not see Sara again until the appointed time when all were to congregate in the drawing room before driving to the theater. He was the first to enter the room and he took up a position below the ornately-framed mirror that hung above the mantelpiece. A fire had been set in the hearth and he passed a few minutes watching, with idle interest, the dancing flames.

He was dressed in his usual manner of conservative elegance; his black coat was exquisitely cut to his broad shoulders; his plain white waistcoat gleamed immaculately by contrast. His shirt points were neither extravagant nor understated, but rose to a perfect height above the complicated arrangement of his neckcloth.

He turned at the sound of the door, and saw Sara enter the room. He straightened, his attention arrested, his gaze firmly fixed upon the picture she created.

She, too, was dressed finely, in a gown of pale pink satin, with buds of silk orchids fashioned into a small nosegay just beneath her bodice. She had, indeed, contrived to put her hair up in a most flattering arrangement and there was a small orchid woven into the careless curls that graced her head like a crown. To Hugh's eyes, which were well trained to appreciate a beautiful woman when they beheld one, Sara looked young and lovely, and exquisitely innocent.

She paused in the center of the room, and she smiled at him rather shyly. "How—how elegant you look!"

His brow went up in a quizzing manner. "May I return the compliment? I have often thought you were too lovely a young woman to be tied to household duties. You have clearly proved me correct!"

"Thank you!" she answered, blushing with pleasure. "I cannot tell you how much I am looking forward to attending the opera." She cast him an earnest look and said, rather tentatively, "I—I am very well aware that I have you to thank for this evening and—and—thank you!"

He smiled slightly. "Not at all. Perhaps you overrate my influence with Carville."

"I do not think so," she said, with a small shake of her head. "Nevertheless, I am grateful to you. I do not know why you agreed to give up your card party in favor of the opera, but I am glad you did!"

"Perhaps I merely wished to see you looking as you do now," he said quietly and again he saw her blush. He didn't think he had ever seen a woman in so becoming a state of confusion. He added, as he moved away from the mantelpiece to where she was standing in the center of the room, "There is only one thing lacking in your appearance, but I believe this shall more than make up for that lapse."

As he spoke, he withdrew from his coat pocket a long, slim box, and he held it out to her. The look in her eye told him how astonished she was; the reluctance with which she accepted the box proved that, however grateful she claimed to be, she did not at all trust him.

She took the box at last and when she opened the lid, she beheld within the velvet lined case the delicately painted fan she had admired in the shop window in town.

Her eyes flew to Hugh's face. "Is—is this for *me?*" she asked, unable to trust her own judgment.

"It is."

"Why?" she asked, clearly suspicious.

"Because you wished for it."

For a long moment, Sara could not decide what to say. Searching his face, she saw no sign of that self-satisfied gleam he had worn the day he had taken her up in his curricle and tried to flirt with her. Neither did she see any indication of the teasing look she had noticed after colliding with him in the corridor. He merely stood, regarding her with perfect gravity, as if her acceptance of such a tribute was of grave importance to him.

She said at last, "Oh, but—but I should not accept such a gift! I am most certain I should not!"

"Do not think of it as a gift," he replied. "Think of it, instead, as a peace offering of sorts. I am trying to prove to you, Sara, that I am not as wicked a fellow as you would believe."

She flushed, once again disconcerted by his direct words and unnerving gaze. "I never thought—surely you are mistaken—" She abandoned all further attempts at coherent speech and dipped her head in embarrassed confusion.

Undeterred, Hugh took the box from between her fingers. He took up the fan and discarded the case on a table. Quite before she knew what he was about, he took Sara's elbow and led her to the mirror that hung above the mantel. He stepped behind her and when he was assured that Sara had a very clear image of herself in the glass, he unfurled the fan and reached around her slim waist to hold it in place before her.

Opened, the fan was just as lovely as she remembered it. There was no denying how well its painted pattern suited her evening gown. Instinctively, Sara's hand clasped the fan and Hugh's hand fell away.

She bit her lip, debating the wisdom of accepting such an offering from a man she had long convinced herself was not worthy of her trust. At last she said, "It—it is a very pretty peace offering. Thank you!"

Hugh stepped away from her then. He had anticipated that she might protest; he had anticipated that she would ultimately accept the gift. What he had not anticipated was his own reaction to her naïve and charming expression of gratitude. Sara was, he realized, a complete innocent. His plans to seduce her, that had withered upon discovering that she was Carville's sister and not his housekeeper, now died within him a sad but gallant death.

Philip entered the room then and exclaimed, "Well, aren't we all in fine looks! I should say we are each quite lovely to behold, yes, indeed!"

He had ordered a chaise for the evening and since it was at that moment drawing up on the drive in front of the house, the little party of theater-goers prepared to leave. Hugh himself handed Sara up into the carriage and took his place beside her.

From his seat opposite, Philip, in excellent humor, caught sight of the painted fan Sara held delicately in her gloved hands. "What's that you've got there," he asked. "That's a new trinket, I think. Very smart! Very smart indeed!"

Sara thanked him for his compliment but in such a muted voice, that she hoped to discourage his asking any further questions about the fan. She was still debating the propriety of having accepted such a gift from Hugh

Deverill, but, truly, she didn't think she had the strength to have refused him.

She could not recall a time when she was ever more charmed by a man than she had been when Hugh had stood behind her and watched her reflection in the mirror. That he was handsome, she had no doubt; that he had treated her with something very akin to kindness while alone with her in the drawing room was something she had not expected. Even less had she expected that she would feel a rather strong tug of attraction for him.

They arrived at the theater to find Lord Westbury and his mother already seated in their box. Sara entered and Lord Westbury jumped to his feet, his smile welcoming; Philip followed, and his lordship bowed low, but when Hugh entered the box, a little behind Philip, his lordship started visibly.

Clearly, his lordship had not expected to see Hugh, but, ever polite, Lord Westbury greeted him, if not with enthusiasm, at least with all that was proper in manner and deportment. He took Sara's hand in his and drew her to where his mother was seated. "Mother, you remember Sara, don't you? Only see how much she has grown since last we saw her!"

Sara dropped a perfect curtsy before Lady Westbury, who ran her eyes over Sara's person in an appraising manner. "So, this is the girl you've been rattling on about for the past three days! Well, stand back and let me have a look at you!" Lady Westbury raised her opera glass, the better to exact another study of her appearance and proclaimed, "Well, you are pretty enough, I should think, although in my day, girls had a bit more meat on them. Back when I was your age, skinny girls weren't at all the fashion, but if you've a mind to attend parties looking for all the world as if you haven't the money to afford a decent meal, that's no business of mine!"

She turned her attention then on Philip and nodded briefly to him, but no sooner did Philip step forward to greet her, than she spied Hugh standing a little in the background. "Bless me, what's *he* doing here?"

Hugh was quite unperturbed to find three pairs of eyes watching him with wide-eyed curiosity. He made his way to Lady Westbury's side and raised her hand to his lips. "I'm staying at the Hall with Carville, ma'am. Once I understood you would be in attendance tonight, I insisted upon coming."

She swatted at his arm. "Don't waste your lovemaking on me, young man! Although I must say, you do it very prettily! Tell me instead how your mother goes on."

Philip, who, along the with rest of the party, overheard this last exchange, repeated in some astonishment, "Your *mother?*"

Hugh cocked one sardonic brow. "Yes. I have one, you know." He returned his attention to Lady Westbury. "My mother was well when last I saw her. I would be happy to convey to her any messages you wish."

Lady Westbury, availing herself of a willing ear, recited a litany of messages and comments for Hugh to pass along when next he found himself in his mother's company. He listened to and remembered only half of them. For all his eyes were trained upon her ladyship's lined and wrinkled face, his attention, throughout that woman's dissertation, remained on Sara. He was acutely aware that she had allowed Westbury to guide her to a chair a good deal apart from where Hugh sat alongside Lady Westbury; he was equally aware that his lordship was an attentive companion. He held Sara's chair for her and handed her his opera glass, adjusting it for her with care.

Hugh turned his attention back to Lady Westbury, and interrupted her catalog of announcements. "Madam, when did you last share a conversation with my mother? I know she would like to see you again."

"It's been years, I dare say, but I still like to think we've remained close. Spends a lot of time in London, doesn't she?"

"She is a famous hostess there, you know."

"Well, and so would I be if my health were any better!" snapped her ladyship.

"I had a notion you were looking quite well," said Hugh, mildly. "Surely you don't come to Bath for the waters, ma'am!"

"Why else would I be in this wretched place?"

"Well, you do have a house here and Westbury is something of a leader of fashion in these parts."

Lady Westbury eyed him critically. "Don't dress the dog in a scarf for my benefit, young man. My son is as dull as a Dutchman, and don't I know it! Sometimes I look at him and wonder that he is truly my own! When I was his age, I was in London creating a stir, not rusticating in Bath, and walking about humming snatches of opera music!"

Hugh was sorely tempted to laugh out loud at that, but said instead, with perfect gravity, "I believe your son is a man of strong principle. He's honest to a fault."

"Honest! Ha! I'd rather he were a little less honest and little more married. It's been years since his wife died, and he ain't shown the least interest in courting a woman."

"I believe he is showing an interest now, ma'am," said Hugh.

Lady Westbury swiveled about in her chair to look down the row to where her son was sitting in earnest conversation with Sara. "Lord, could it be?" she asked of no one in particular. She turned back toward Hugh. "He could do worse than Sara. She's a good girl. I knew her parents, of course. Fine people of good families, but they're long gone and buried. That brother of hers, though, is a bit of a rapscallion and I wouldn't trust him to do right by her. Tell me, how is it that you have come to stay at the manor?''

"I came at the invitation of the rapscallion," said Hugh.

"Is that so? Well, I can't say that I'm surprised, for you've always been something of a rogue, yourself!"

"You flatter me, ma'am," said Hugh, as the curtain went up and the first chords of music filled the theater.

He turned slightly in his chair, the better to see the stage, but he found, instead, that he was afforded a clear view of Sara's profile as she viewed the opera. There was no mistaking the delight in her expression as she watched the players on the stage and he found himself much more entertained by her reaction to the performance than he was by the performance itself.

As he watched Sara's animated expression, Hugh was struck again by the fact that she was much more innocent than most women of his acquaintance. Innocent, too, was she of her situation, for he doubted very much that she was at all concerned with the fact that she was the only female, save a handful of servants, in a house full of men.

Had she lived alone with only her brother, such an arrangement would have been quite unexceptional, but with Hugh and Jasper Hetherington in residence, even for a short length of time, Sara should have had the protection of a chaperone. At the least, she should have had a lady's maid to lend her some small amount of credibility. But being the innocent that she was, such thoughts had, he was sure, never occurred to her.

Nor had such thoughts occurred to her scapegrace of a brother. In fact, Hugh was heartily convinced that Philip hadn't given a single thought to his sister's reputation; even less had Philip considered that by setting her up as a servant in the house, he had placed Sara in a rather compromising situation. An employee was not, after all, entitled to the same protection as the daughter of the establishment. While Hugh was gratified to think that he had not really behaved in any more coming fashion toward Sara than a mild flirtation, he was a little alarmed to think how far he might have gone had he still thought her to be nothing more than the housekeeper.

At the intermission, their party broke up for a short time. Lady Westbury rose to her feet immediately once the curtain fell upon the stage and demanded that her son escort her out for a breath of air and an opportunity to stretch her legs. Philip followed them, intent upon procuring some refreshments for himself and Sara. Hugh slipped easily into the chair Lord Westbury had vacated and asked, politely, "Are you enjoying the performance?"

"I am indeed!" said Sara, promptly, her eyes still aglow from the excitement of the evening. "Lord Westbury has very kindly interpreted the entire opera for me. My Italian, I'm afraid, is not very good, but I am enjoying the dramatics no less because of it."

"I'm glad," said Hugh. "Perhaps, if you had someone who shared your interests, you might find that you could attend the theater or the opera more often. Tell me, Sara, is there no one—no female relative, for instance—who might come and stay with you at Carvington Hall?"

Surprised, Sara turned to him. "Why, no! Why do you ask?"

"No reason," he said, smoothly. Perceiving that she was still regarding him with a look of wary curiosity, he lied, quite neatly. "I am merely concerned that you have been working much too hard. It occurred to me that another lady in the house might be able to take some of the burden off you."

Sara wondered over his concern, but as Lord Westbury returned then with his mother and Philip arrived bearing a glass of punch which he delivered to her with much pleasure, she was given no opportunity to ask him what he meant by such a comment.

Hugh returned to his seat as the curtain rose on the second act, and Sara gave his odd question no more thought. It was happiness enough that she was at last enjoying at least one of the entertainments the Bath season had to offer.

When at last the curtain rang down on the final scene and the opera was at last concluded, Sara drew a contented breath. Lord Westbury cast her a benevolent look, saying, "I knew you should enjoy it."

"I cannot think when I have delighted in anything more. It was beautiful! Simply beautiful! Thank you so very much for inviting me—all of us!—to join you!"

"It was my pleasure, Sara. I shall hope you will oblige me by accepting another of my invitations in the future." He took her hand as he spoke, and held it fast for a moment. "I, too, cannot remember when I have enjoyed myself more."

Sara felt the heat of a blush mantle her cheeks. She was far from experienced in the ways of men, but she knew very well that Lord Westbury was paying particular attention to her and she wasn't quite sure how she should react. Slowly, she withdrew her hand from his.

He said, "I think I just saw my mother disguise a very polite yawn behind the back of her hand. She is not used to late hours, I'm afraid. I think it is time I returned her home. But first, I should like to have your permission to call upon you."

"Of course!" she said, politely. "I hope you will call very soon."

He cast her a fleeting smile, then turned to Lady Westbury. "Mother, I believe it is time we bid our guests goodnight."

"If you think we must, although lord knows I ain't tired."

She held her hand out to Hugh. "Deverill, I charge you to call upon me tomorrow and relate to me all the scandals you've been causing since last I saw you! No, don't deny it, for a greater rogue than you never drew a breath! Mark me, now! Tomorrow! I shall take it very ill if you should fail me!"

"It shall be my pleasure," said Hugh, bowing over her hand.

Thus, the theater party broke up and each party went their separate ways. On the carriage ride back to Carvington Hall, Sara's head was filled with happy visions of the theater performance and contented feelings for everyone with whom she had spent the evening. Curiously, she was feeling most at charity with Hugh. She was intelligent enough to know that without him, there would have been no visit to the opera, no flattering experience of having an attentive man such as Lord Westbury at her side, and, perhaps most importantly, no delicately painted fan.

She was very well aware that he had given up his card party in order to ensure she was able to attend the performance. For what reason he had done so, she could not guess, but several times during the evening, while the players were onstage and the attention of the audience was fixed upon their doings, she had felt Hugh's eyes upon her.

She knew that she had been looking her best; she had spent hours on her *toilette* and gown, and she had very much wanted Hugh to think her pretty. He had paid her some very nice compliments in the drawing room earlier, but she had found herself wanting more from him. She wanted to feel again that tug of attraction, that electric shock she had experienced when he had held her in his arms in the gallery. She thought she might at last have it when he had taken Lord Westbury's chair and he had attempted to engage her in conversation.

But his words had been far from the lover-like murmurings she had hoped for. Instead of complimenting her, he had asked after her relatives. Even worse, when he might have flirted with her and reduced her to a state of exhilarating breathlessness as he had so often before, he had instead told her that she was working too hard, reminding her, in the most disappointing way, that he thought her no more than an employee of Carvington Hall.

Lord Westbury, on the other hand, had been quite attentive; Sara could not resist the niggling feeling he was a little bit attracted to her. He had left the theater with the promise that he would call upon her very soon and Sara did not for a moment doubt that he would find some excuse to visit her the very next day.

Chapter Ten

Sara was in her sitting room the next afternoon, busily arranging a vase of flowers when Daisy presented to her a silver tray bearing Lord Westbury's card.

She went down to the drawing room immediately and held out her hand to him. "My lord, I fear you find me all alone. My brother is out riding at the moment, but I assure you, had he known you intended to visit, he would have made a point of being here."

"Tell him I am sorry to have missed him," said Lord Westbury, with the manners for which he was famed, "although I must admit that I had hoped to be able to speak with you alone."

Sara felt herself blushing and tried to dispel her sudden unease. "Please sit down. And please allow me to tell you again how much I—we—enjoyed your theater party last night."

He sat down next to her and looked at her with a seriousness that quite captured her attention. "Sara, I—forgive me, but I have something to say to you! We have known each other so long and so well for enough years that I presume our friendship allows us certain liberties. Sara, I did not call this afternoon merely to be sociable. You see, I am here to ensure your safety."

"My—my safety?" she repeated, astonished.

"Your welfare has weighed heavily on my heart during the last week," he said, most earnestly, "ever since I learned that you had guests staying here at the Hall. Tell me truthfully, Sara: are-are you quite *well*?"

She laughed slightly, and gave her head a small shake of confusion. "Of course I am well! Why should I not be?"

"Because of your situation here with—because of your position—" He stopped short, perceiving the look of bewilderment on her face. "Sara, must I speak plainly to you?"

She laughed again. "I am rather afraid you shall have to! Truly, Lord Westbury, I do not know what you mean."

"I am speaking of Deverill and Hetherington! Bluntly put, I am concerned for your safety as long as those men remain in this house."

Those words quite took the wind from Sara's sails. She looked at Lord Westbury a long moment before replying. "Sir, I cannot understand you. Should I not be ever more safe with *three* men in the house to protect me from whatever dangers you imagine?"

"Not when one of the men himself poses the danger!" said his lordship. He clasped her hand in an urgent grip. "Sara, there is a reason the man is known as Devil Deverill."

Again, she was quiet a moment. At last she said, in a tight little voice, "I am well aware, sir, that Mr. Deverill gambles and I believe he is no stranger to drink, though in my presence he has never over-indulged."

Now it was Lord Westbury's chance to laugh, but he did so kindly. "My sweet Sara, you are dearly innocent! I wish it did not fall to me to teach you that the world is full of people who are not as kind and virtuous as you. Sadly, Deverill is just one such person."

Sara did not know what to say, but she was suddenly struck by an almost overwhelming desire to defend Hugh Deverill. She said, with a feeling of confusion mixed with alarm, "Sir, I cannot understand your meaning. I beg you to speak plain with me!"

"Very well," he said, tightening his hold on her hand, "I shall apprise you of the kind of man he is and I can only hope you may forgive me for saying so. I did not come here to warn you of Deverill's gambling or drinking. Those are, I hope, vices of his that could never cause you any harm. No, dear Sara, it is Deverill's conduct with women that concerns me and makes me fear for your safety."

Sara felt her breath catch in her throat. "His—his conduct with women?" she repeated, faintly. "What—what do you know of it?"

"I know his reputation with females runs the length and breadth of England," said Westbury. "He has, I believe, no preference for high-born ladies over tavern serving wenches. He can ravish a chambermaid as easily and with little more conscience than he would pinch a housekeeper. In general, he conducts himself with the worst possible principles and the lowest of morals."

"No! No, I cannot bring myself to believe such things!" said Sara, snatching her hand from within his grasp and bounding to her feet.

Lord Westbury looked at her sadly and rose from his chair. "I know you think he can be a charming fellow. Why, I saw evidence of it myself last night! But do not let Deverill fool you, Sara. He is quite cunning, especially when it comes to seducing women."

She stared at him, her eyes wide and the protest she had been about to utter dying upon her lips. She said, quite faintly, "S—seducing women?"

"I beg your pardon! I should not have spoken so! I had intended to be delicate and infinitely patient, but I have shocked you instead!"

"Indeed you have!" she said, sinking slowly down upon the chair again. "Tell me, has Mr. Deverill had many flirts?"

"Countless, I'm afraid."

"I see." She turned her head away, wishing with all her might that Lord Westbury had never presented himself at Carvington Hall. "I—I can hardly believe it."

"Of course! I understand! It is too horrid for you to believe, but you may trust me to always speak the truth to you, Sara, and to always try to provide you the benefits of my wisdom and years."

Sara was quite certain that the benefits of which he spoke were quite non-existent in this case. She was on her feet in an instant. "No, Lord Westbury! You are wrong! You are, I am certain, most heartily wrong!"

"Sara, you are goodness itself to want to defend a man of Deverill's ilk," he said, casting her a look of worried concern, "but I shall not think less of you for acknowledging the truth about his character."

She moved with some agitation about the room, fighting with all her might the charges Lord Westbury had made concerning Hugh Deverill. Hugh was not a man she could claim to know very well, for theirs was an acquaintance of short duration. But she knew in her heart that Hugh was nothing like the man Westbury had just described. She could not condone Hugh's influence over Philip, but she had never before seen him behave in as depraved a fashion as had just been portrayed to her.

On the contrary; she had, since the moment of their meeting, found Hugh Deverill to be a man of considerable charm. She had witnessed for herself that he had the capacity to behave with surprising tenderness where she was concerned.

And so she considered telling Lord Westbury, but before she could form the words to defend Hugh, Lord Westbury was again at her side, clasping her hand in a most compelling grip.

"Sara, my dear, I have distressed you! Please know that was never my intent!"

"I—I know you mean well," she said, but she was feeling most distressed indeed. "Of course I know it was not your intent to shock me, but you must know, too, that Mr. Deverill—"

"Sara," he interrupted, in a kindly voice, "I would be very pleased if you would come to Bath to stay. You shall be a welcome guest in my home and you shall have my mother, of course, for companionship."

She looked at him sharply. "Are—are you asking me to come and—and *live* with you?"

"For as long as you wish," he answered, promptly.

His words surprised another laugh of confusion from her. "But—but my home is here! Why, pray, should you wish me to leave it?"

He could have given her a dozen reasons why, but Lord Westbury was of the opinion that she would not have understood a one of them. He had never before found himself in the delicate position of having to explain to a properly-nurtured young lady that by remaining in her own home, she was residing in the lion's den. That, he knew, was no exaggeration, for he considered Hugh Deverill a predator of the highest order when it came to females. He wished most heartily that he had the courage to say just so to Sara, but one look in her blue eyes, gone wide with innocent confusion, and the words died away on his lips.

Still possessing himself of her hand, he said, instead, very gently, "Sara, is there not someone then who might be in the way of staying with you here at Carvington Hall? Some female relative who might come here to live?''

That question, she thought, sounded vaguely familiar. In fact, it sounded very much like a similar question Hugh had posed to her the very night before. "Someone to stay?'' she repeated. "What do you mean? Why do you ask?''

"My dear girl, you are not making this easy on me!'' said Westbury, in a rueful tone. "I am speaking of another woman—perhaps a woman of gracefully older years. A relative will do, or even an old nurse or governess—a woman who will, in short, lend you a bit of countenance and preserve your reputation.''

Sara stared at him a moment, hardly able to credit that he had echoed almost the very words that Hugh had spoken to her. "But, my brother resides here with me, as well.''

"I'm afraid that once other bachelors were introduced into the house, your brother's presence was no longer sufficient to protect you. You need another female, a woman of years and social cache, to preserve your reputa-tion, Sara. Failing that, you should leave the house, or your guests must leave. I'm sorry I must be the one to bring such matters to you. I only wish someone had considered all this on your behalf.''

But Sara had a sneaking suspicion that someone had done just so. Incredibly, she was filled with the notion that Hugh Deverill had been thinking very much the same thing when he had asked after Sara's welfare the night before. She hadn't expected such gallantry from him and her heart swelled with the notion that he had taken such care with her. It was all she could do to concentrate on Lord Westbury's visit instead of wandering off to another room and ponder on her own the meaning behind Hugh's extraordinary behavior but she managed it somehow.

And when Lord Westbury was at last gone and she was afforded a few moments alone, Sara realized that she was perilously close to losing her heart to Hugh Deverill. She didn't know why, for she half suspected that all the horrid things Lord Westbury had relayed concerning his conduct were very probably true.

But when she thought of his words to her the night before, when she considered how he had spoken to her about her living arrangements, all the while wishing to protect her from himself and the damage he might cause her, she realized she had been fortunate to see a side of him that others, such as Lord Westbury, had not been privileged to see.

She was, indeed, on a fair course to losing her heart and she didn't quite know what to do about it. She had never been in love before, and she was seized with an overwhelming desire to speak of her emotions with someone. Just as she had in her days as a child, when she had confided to him all her many fantasies and dreams, Sara went in search of her brother.

She quickly discovered that Philip was nowhere to be found in the house, but she did discover Daisy who, as usual, proved to be a treasure trove of information concerning the men of her orbit. Sara had merely to mention to her that she could not find her Philip anywhere and the maid quite happily relayed to her any and all her knowledge concerning Philip's whereabouts.

"I suspect," said Daisy, "he was bound for the stables."

"Did you see him go in that direction?"

"No, but he was dressed for riding, and looking fine as fivepence—as were the two London gentlemen, I should say. Quite handsome they all were; handsome enough to make me wish I had some duties as would take me to the stables, too."

That comment summoned a smile from Sara but her heart was too troubled to laugh, as she normally did, over Daisy's maxims regarding men.

When Sara arrived at the stables, all was quiet and the place looked quite empty. As with the rest of the servants, the stable boys, grooms, and coachmen had left Carvington Hall long ago when Philip had stopped paying their wages. As the majority of Philip's horses had been sold over time for the amount of cash they would bring to pay expenses and provide some little upkeep on the manor, there were, except for one or two of Philip's favorite hunters, few horses left within the stalls.

Like the rest of the manor, the stables suffered from neglect and looked nothing like the stables of Sara's memory. The painted walls showed signs of cracking and peeling and she thought the hay looked far from fresh. The floors were in need of cleaning and, judging from the number of flies and the odor that hung about the place, it had been too long since last the floor had been washed.

The stables were quiet upon her arrival. For a moment she thought her search for Philip would prove futile, but a slight sound from the far stall attracted her attention.

"Easy, boy," came Hugh's voice from a stall on the other side of a dividing half-wall. "Easy, now."

Sara started. After Lord Westbury's revelations, and the stirrings of her own heart, Hugh Deverill was the last man she wished to see. Before she could make a hasty and unobserved retreat, Hugh appeared from around the corner of the stall.

He had removed his coat and cravat and his waistcoat was loosed and his sleeves rolled up to his elbows. He was leading a magnificent black stallion of sixteen hands that fretted slightly and showed every sign of posing a challenge to Hugh's muscled hold on him.

Hugh walked the animal around a bit, his attention so fixed upon the horse that he did not see her at first. Then he looked at her, and exclaimed, "Sara! I had no notion you were here! What brings you?"

"I am looking for my—for Lord Carville. I must speak with him on a matter of some importance."

"He's not here; he's out riding with Hetherington. I should be there myself, but my horse scraped a fetlock."

She took a tentative step toward him. "Is it very bad?"

"No, I don't think so, but it must be dressed." He murmured something soothing to the horse and rubbed his hand down the length of the animal's neck. After a few minutes of such attention, the horse calmed considerably.

That he had a way with horses was not a surprise to Sara, for Philip had told her once that Hugh Deverill was a bruising rider and noted whipster of the Corinthian set. She had never supposed that he would condescend to care for his animals himself, but he proved her wrong.

There was a gentleness about him as he lifted the animal's leg and examined its wound. His long fingers tentatively probed up and down the horse's fetlock, seeking out tenderness, yet careful not to cause the animal any more discomfort or pain. Watching him, she recalled quite vividly the feeling of Hugh's hand across the small of her back when he had danced with her that evening in the long gallery. Those same strong, tapered fingers that moved so nimbly down the horse's leg had once spread possessively across the back of her waist.

"Hand me that ointment, will you?" he asked, stretching his arm out toward her. She saw the bottle he needed and passed it to him. His hand, when he took the bottle, brushed lightly against her fingers. Compared to her own hand, his seemed huge; his wrist was thick and his forearm was muscled beneath its light dusting of hair. He had at that moment the look about him of a laborer, tanned and strong, and used to wielding his strength.

She watched him in open admiration for a moment, then asked, "Is it difficult for you to care for your horses without a groom or stable boy?"

"It's a cursed nuisance, is what it is," he said, in a tone mixed of amusement and exasperation. "How the devil does Carville manage?"

"Not very well, I'm afraid," said Sara, her expressive eyes traveling once again over the poor condition of the stables. "I dare say I might be in the way of engaging a stable boy as soon as I receive my quarter-day allowance."

No sooner did the words leave her lips than she realized her error. She blushed fiercely and waited for Hugh to question why a housekeeper should expect to receive a lady's allowance.

But the question never came. Instead, Hugh continued to concentrate on the animal's leg. After a moment, Sara relaxed slightly and realized that, except for Philip, she had never before seen a man with his coat off and his shirt sleeves rolled up so. In Hugh, she thought the effect was quite handsome. The tanned skin of his neck disappeared beneath the snowy white of his shirt collar as it lay open; and the thin material of his shirt could not hide the breadth of his strong shoulders as they worked gently over the animal.

Spying a length of clean linen that was lying alongside Hugh's coat and cravat, Sara picked it up. "Is this what you mean to use to bandage the wound?"

He glanced at her. "Yes, it is, but—"

"I can be of help to you then," she said, promptly. "I once helped a groom make bandages for a pony that had frisked against a fence and scraped his shoulder on the wood."

She took up the linen, then, and began to rip it into neat lengths.

"Sara, there is no need for you to do that," he said, pausing in his labors.

"But I can help you." She tore another strip from the fabric with determination.

"Sara. Sara!" he cried, a bit more forcibly. Heedless, she continued to rip the bandage lengths until he went to her and grasped her hands to still them. "Sara, I don't need your help."

"Nonsense!" she said, with a slight laugh. "I should be glad to help. Only look at the bandages I have made!"

"No, Sara," he said in such a stern tone that she could not fail to heed him. "Sara, you must go back to the house now. Don't you know you shouldn't be alone here with me?"

"Why?" she asked, looking him full in the eye. "Because you might try to seduce me?"

For a moment he was too astounded to speak. "I suppose I might guess where you heard that," he said, frowning. "Westbury has been busy. No, Sara, you may rest easy. I shall not try to seduce you."

She fought back a niggling sense of disappointment. "Do you *promise* you shall not seduce me?"

He raised his hand, as if he were taking an oath. "Upon my honor."

"In that case, then, I have nothing to fear and I may stay and help without consideration for what may happen."

"It isn't a question of what may happen between us, Sara. It is a question of what people *think* may have happened between us."

"I'm quite surprised to hear you say so. I always thought, you see, that you were a man who didn't care what others may say of you."

"For the most part, it's true, but that is a decision I can only make for myself. I cannot make that judgment for you."

"Why?" she asked, in a slightly breathless voice.

He looked at her a long moment and wondered if he had what it took to play this game of flirtation with an innocent. "If I have to explain the rules to you, you are much too young to play the game. It is time you went back to the house, anyway."

"May I not stay here with you?"

"No, you may not." He took her hand and led her to the stable door.

"I could help you bandage the horse's leg," she offered, clearly reluctant to leave.

"I shall manage to do so on my own."

"But what if you need assistance? What if you need someone to hand you something, just as I handed you the bottle of ointment a few minutes ago?"

"I am possessed of two arms that extend from my shoulders all the way to the tips of my fingers. Believe me, I am able to reach whatever I need."

Sara laughed as they came to a stop just inside the stable door. There, in the light of the late afternoon sun, with the lights of her hair shining like gold, and her lips parted in a happy smile, Hugh thought she looked lovelier than he had yet seen her.

It was difficult indeed for him to release her hand and take a deliberate step back, but he did so. He would have rather taken her in his arms and kissed her until he heard again her breath come to her in short little bursts. Had she been any other woman of his acquaintance, he might have done so, but she was Miss Sara Brandon-Howe, the refreshingly innocent daughter of Carvington Hall; the same Miss Sara Brandon-Howe who had somehow stirred in him a sense of nobility where she was concerned.

He called upon that nobility now, as he stood there, fighting against an impulse to kiss her.

"What is it? Why do you look at me so?" she asked, her head cocked slightly to one side as she looked up at him.

The impulse surged in strength. "I was merely wondering . . ."

"Yes? Wondering what?"

"I was wondering what you would do if I kissed you just now," he said, recognizing with barely a fight the superior strength of impulse over nobility.

He saw her lips part slightly in surprise, and the impulse gained a measure of strength. Slowly, he held out his hand until his fingers brushed the smoothness of her cheek. He took a step toward her, then he tucked his fingers beneath her chin and tilted her head back.

Sara didn't fight him; indeed, she could hardly move, so mesmerized was she by the prospect of being kissed by Hugh Deverill. She wanted him to kiss her more than anything she had ever wanted in her life; and, almost impatiently, she waited for his lips to touch hers.

Slowly, as if he were half afraid he might frighten her, Hugh bent toward her. He took his time, watching her reaction, savoring the manner in which her lashes fluttered slightly as he moved ever closer to her, and the manner in which her breath caught so becomingly between her lips.

He brushed her mouth lightly with his own and drew back a little, the better to enjoy her reaction. But as he lifted his head, as he prepared to kiss her again with decidedly more passion, he heard the scuffling sound of horses and men approaching.

Kissing Sara, with all its attending sweetness, would have to wait, for in the next moment, Lord Hetherington and Jim Cotton appeared in the stable yard, and between them they half-dragged an obviously injured Philip.

Chapter Eleven

"What is it? What has happened?" asked Sara as the men half-dragged Philip into the stable.

With an expression bordering on disgust, Lord Hetherington deposited Philip upon the stable floor. "The clumsy pup fell off his horse! I never saw such a spectacle!"

"My goodness!" breathed Sara, fearing the worst. She knelt beside her brother and clutched his lifeless hand. A quick examination told her that his complexion was pale, his lips were drawn into a tight line, and his blue eyes were closed against the pain. "Philip! Philip, dear! Are you injured? Are you conscious? Speak to me!"

"Ahhh, he be all right, ma'am," said Hugh's tiger, Jim Cotton. "He's injured his foot, is all. Looks like a nasty sprain about the ankle, but nothing broken, I dare say."

Sara saw that her brother's boot had been removed and that his stockinged foot was quite swollen. "Philip? Philip, what happened?"

He opened one bleary eye and retorted in a voice that

slurred slightly, "How in blue blazes should I know? I was riding along, nice as you please, when suddenly I was on one side of a jump and my blasted horse was on the other!"

Sara looked up at first Hetherington, then Jim. "Jump? What jump?"

"The jump he insisted upon taking," said Lord Hetherington, with a distinct lack of sympathy. "Of course, *I* recommended that he not attempt it! Any sapskull could see it was dangerous. *I* saw in an instant that the hedgerow by the lake was much too high and steep where it approaches the west end."

"The hedgerow by the lake? But Philip has taken that jump countless times!" said Sara.

"And I would have made it again," uttered Philip, "if I weren't drunk as a wheelbarrow!"

Sara looked at him in disbelief. "Drunk?" she repeated, quite unable to believe her ears. *"Drunk?* Philip Brandon-Howe, do you mean to tell me—"

"I think," interceded Hugh, "it would be a good idea to get Carville to bed. Give me a hand, will you Hetherington?"

He stepped in front of Sara as he spoke and pulled Philip up beside him. By slipping an arm about Philip's waist he and Lord Hetherington managed to half-carry, half-drag Philip into the house and up the stairs to his bedchamber.

Sara gathered up Philip's cast-off boot and hurried ahead to open the doors and clear the way. In her brother's room, she turned back the bed clothes and Hugh carefully settled Philip upon the bed.

"Let me help," said Sara, rushing to arrange some pillows behind Philip.

"Begging your pardon, madam," said Jim Cotton, "but his lordship would be better served if you was to put the pillows under his foot instead."

"Are you quite certain?" she asked, with a doubtful frown. "Won't he be more comfortable with the cushions behind his head?"

"No, madam," said the tiger, "on account of the swelling. I have had some experience with these things and I think you'll find the injury will heal faster if we put it up and let some of the poisons drain away. We'll settle him with a nice hot brick, madam, and he'll be much more comfortable."

"Poisons?" repeated Sara, casting an alarmed look toward her brother's pale and haggard face. "I—I think it would be best if we sent for a doctor!"

"If that is what you wish, Sara," said Hugh, "then a doctor shall be fetched. In the meantime, why don't you wait downstairs while we do our best to make Carville more comfortable?"

"Leave him? I—I couldn't! He needs me!"

"At the moment, I dare say he doesn't even recognize you. He won't miss you if you were to leave the room for a bit while we strip him and put him to bed. I'm afraid you are shockingly in the way, Sara."

She clasped her brother's hand, saying defiantly, "I wouldn't dream of leaving him now! Philip, dear, don't fret; I promise everything shall be well. I shall be with you day and night, if need be." When she received no response to these words of devotion, she bent over him, saying gently, "Philip, dear? Did you hear me?"

Her brother opened one muzzy eye and, after a moment's examination of her face, said, "Oh, give over, Peg, and sing another chorus, eh?"

Startled, Sara drew back and looked at Hugh. "Who is Peg?"

Philip obligingly enlightened her, mumbling, "And have the barkeep fill my glass again, Peg. There's a dear!"

Her back went suddenly rigid and her expression was

disapproving. "What is he talking about? What does this mean?"

"It means it is time you left," said Hugh. He disengaged her hand from Philip's and gently guided her toward the door. "I have no doubt you are an excellent nurse, but in this instance, you shall have to leave the men to care for the invalid."

She shook off his hand. "Nothing short of force could make me leave his side!"

"As you wish," responded Hugh, politely. "But I rather think that if I were to pick you up in my arms and carry you out of here, as enjoyable as I may find the task, Carville might find the commotion a little unsettling."

His tone was quite even as he spoke those words, but Sara thought there was also a rather flinty light within the depths of Hugh's grey eyes that told her he was quite capable of carrying out such a threat.

She put up her chin and directed a rather stubborn look toward each occupant of the room. "Very well! I shall go, but only because you leave me little choice!"

He smiled slightly and said with infuriating kindness, "I shall come to you presently in the drawing room with news of the patient."

But he didn't come as quickly as Sara would have liked. In fact, she waited what seemed a very long time—hours, perhaps—before Hugh at last made an appearance. During her vigil she was given ample opportunity to imagine the worst and allow her nimble mind to run rampant and invent visions of the most odious fate for her brother.

She was pacing the length of the drawing room when Hugh at last came in. She barely allowed him time to close the door before she went to him, saying anxiously, "I heard the doctor arrive quite some time ago. Is—is he very badly injured? Shall he ever recover?"

"I dare say he shall recover enough to plague you with

more of his mischief very soon,'' said Hugh, gently. He took one of her slim hands in his and led her toward a small settee set near the window. He sat down beside her. ''Carville is resting comfortably. Between Lambert and Jim Cotton, someone will remain with him all night.''

''But—but is he badly hurt?''

''You have nothing to fear, Sara. Except for his pride, he has injured nothing seriously.''

''Thank heavens!'' she said, with great relief. ''When I saw him lying on that dreadful stable floor, I thought—! Well, I shall not tell you what I thought! But, are you quite certain he is not seriously maimed? He won't be crippled or suffer a lifetime of great pain, will he? What, if you please, are the nature of his injuries?''

Hugh smiled slightly. ''They are just as Jim Cotton said: a sprained ankle, a few bumps and bruises—nothing more.''

''Are you certain?''

''Very much so. The doctor confirmed it.'' He saw the faint line of worry disappear from her brow and said, compellingly, ''Sara, Carville shall be well, I promise you! He shall be up and about and back to his old self within a fortnight.''

''Thank heaven!''

His smile softened. ''I am glad I could ease your mind.''

''May I see him?''

''I think not. The doctor has given him a potion to help him sleep. Wait until the morning to see him, Sara. I dare say he shall be glad of your company then.'' He looked at her a long moment, then possessed himself of her hand again and held it between the strength of his own two hands. ''Sara, I am at your disposal. If there is anything you need, you have merely to call on me.''

Surprised, she looked up into his grey eyes and saw there a gentleness, a look of kind concern she had never before seen there. That look, coupled with the sincerity of his words and the low, beguiling tone of voice he had used, had the effect of sending her heart beating a good deal faster. Her fingers fluttered nervously within his grasp and she said, in a voice that sounded surprisingly breathless, even to her own ears, "You—you are a good deal too kind, sir!"

"Am I? You're the first person who has ever said so, I assure you. Don't start imagining me to be the hero in this tragedy when I could just as easily behave as the villain."

"You have never acted so before where I was concerned."

He cast her an odd little smile. "Haven't I? I wonder why?"

That question, however, was to remain unanswered, for the door to the drawing room opened and Lord Hetherington entered. "Deverill, I have quite made up my mind that we should—" He stopped short, suddenly aware that he had stumbled upon a rather cozy scene. "I beg your pardon! Shall I leave?"

Slowly, Hugh released Sara's hand and rose to his feet. "Not at all," he said smoothly, but Sara saw in an instant that his mood had changed. Gone was the gentleness from his eyes and the easy grace of his movements. Instead, he stood a trifle stiffly, and looked back at Lord Hetherington with a wary expression.

His abrupt change made her uncomfortable and she, too, rose. "I have some work to attend. I'll leave you now, I think. Thank you again, Mr. Deverill, for your kind assistance today."

With infinite politeness, Lord Hetherington held the door for her. No sooner had she quit the room and he had closed the door again, than his lordship turned to cast a sharp look at Hugh.

Hugh ignored him and crossed the room to stand at a window that offered a view of Carvington Hall's parklands.

He stood there a moment, his attention on the pastoral scene before him, then said, "You were, I think, about to tell me that you had made up your mind about something."

"Yes—yes, I have!" said his lordship. "I've decided I've had just about enough of Carville's shabby notion of hospitality and I should hazard a guess that you have, too. I've begun making arrangements for us to leave today—now!"

Hugh looked around, one brow cocked questioningly. "Us?"

"I can have my bags packed within the hour, if you'll allow me your man Lambert to help. We can be gone from here by nightfall, and take decent lodgings in Bath for a night or two until we can remove to London."

Hugh turned his attention back to the view outside the window. "You have everything planned, I see."

"Well, there is no sense in prolonging our torture! Everything about Carville and his manners is cheese-paring, to say the least. We should have left this wretched place when first we realized Carville's pockets were to let. And today, when he made a cake of himself in the field—I tell you, a man can take only so much of such nonsense! I'll tell Lambert to start packing, Deverill."

"I shouldn't be too quick about it, if I were you. I won't be leaving, you see. But, please, be my guest—use Lambert's talents to pack your things, if you like."

Lord Hetherington stared at him a moment. "What's got into you, Deverill?"

"I cannot think what you mean. I am as I always was."

"You're nothing like yourself! Since the moment we arrived at this god-forsaken place, we've seen nothing but discomfort and cheerless accommodations from a host who is little more than a pauper! And yet, you've said nothing! You've *done* nothing."

"What would you have me do?"

"Leave, for one thing! There is nothing to keep you here!"

Hugh was silent for a moment. Then he said, quietly, "I can't leave now, Hetherington. She needs me."

"*She?*" repeated his lordship, in an incredulous tone. "You're talking of the housekeeper again, aren't you? A servant!"

"Sara is not a servant—I told you that before."

"Well, she certainly isn't a princess in disguise!" uttered Lord Hetherington, sarcastically. "I'll tell you what she is: she's a housekeeper who has made a Charlie of you, and the worst of it is that you don't seem to care!"

"I suggest you mind your tongue, Hetherington," said Hugh, with deadly calm.

"Why? Because you cannot abide hearing the truth? Well, the truth of the matter is that you're being made to look like a load of cobblers, all because of a housekeeper!"

"My actions," said Hugh ominously, "have nothing to do with any of Carville's employees."

"Haven't they? Then let me remind you of the reason we came to Bath in the first place! We came because you were of a mind to fleece Black Jack Hardy in a card game. We came because there was entertainment to be had in the gentlemen's quarters in town. We came," he continued, angrily, "because Carville promised us agreeable accommodations and some excellent riding, all in close proximity to Bath. Instead, we arrived here to find an unkempt, run-down manor house that afforded us not the least comfort. Worse, we missed Hardy's card party in favor of watching an insipid performance at a second-rate opera house! Explain that, if you can!"

But Hugh could not explain it nor did he wish to try. For to explain his actions, he would have had to examine his motives for behaving as he did, and he didn't think he wanted to do that yet. He didn't think he wanted to con-

sider that since the moment he had first set eyes upon
Miss Sara Brandon-Howe, he had done little else but think
of ways in which to please her. Not for a moment did he
consider that she was any other but Carville's sister. Why
she might have agreed to have posed as a mere servant in
her own household, he could only guess. He did know,
however, that her scamp of a brother was leading her a
dance and he wished only to shield her from its consequences.

He had never before felt quite so protective of another
person. Perhaps it was her innocence that touched him,
or perhaps it was her obvious lack of guile and an inability
to lie that made him wish to save her from the folly of her
own actions. No matter the reason, he found that he was
genuinely concerned for Sara; concerned because her reputation was at risk by remaining in a bachelor household
without so much as a chaperone; concerned because he
greatly feared her brother would lead her to ruin; and
concerned that the next time he held her in his arms, he
wouldn't be satisfied to stop with a mere kiss.

He considered the fact that by admitting such, he was
just as guilty of wishing to take advantage of her as her
rapscallion of a brother. Now that Philip was confined to
bed, he knew that Sara was utterly defenseless against the
murmurs of the town tabbies and his own advances.

But it was beyond his power to admit such a thing to
himself, let alone to Jasper Hetherington. Hugh looked
across the room at his friend. "I'll explain nothing, Hetherington. If you mean to leave, I shall wish you good
journey."

"So that's it? That's your intent—to follow about behind
a servant girl like a lap dog? I should never have thought
it of you! Never in a million years!"

"I am not at all certain I understand it myself," said
Hugh, from his place by the window.

"We've been friends for years, and I still cannot say I understand you! I only wish you would see sense and leave this place."

"I'm sure I shall, but not now."

"Well, I, for one, have had enough of Carville's cold comfort! I'm taking a room in Bath for the next few days, then I'm bound for London! When you have at last come to your senses, and wish for some decent companionship, I shall see you there!"

Chapter Twelve

Sara took Hugh's advice and waited until the next morning to pay her visit to Philip's sick room. She hesitated a moment outside the door but when she heard some activity on the other side, she knocked softly and opened the door just wide enough to allow her to peek around it.

"Philip? Are you awake? May—may I come in?"

Her brother didn't answer, but Jim Cotton did. He had passed the night on a truckle bed in the corner of the room and had yet to leave Philip's side since the accident. He opened the door wide enough for her to pass through. "Good morning, madam. I'm just tidying up and shall be gone presently. I'm sure his lordship could do with a bit of comfort this morning."

She looked over at her Philip. He was propped up in bed against an assembly of pillows; his eyes were closed and his complexion was pale and rather pasty; and there was a definite frown across his brow that caused her immediate concern.

"Perhaps I should come back later? When he is feeling more the thing?"

"No, madam, I believe he could do with a bit of cheer this morning. If you'll stay with him for a moment or two, I might fetch him some breakfast and see if he won't eat a bite."

"Of course I shall stay. Yes, thank you, Jim! I'm sure Lord Carville could do with something to eat."

Jim closed the door as he left, leaving Sara in the still quiet of the sick room and unsure what to do next. Philip remained motionless beneath the coverlet, looking small and ridiculously boyish against the vast expanse of the oversized four-poster bed.

"Philip? Are you awake?" she asked, softly.

He stirred then and opened his eyes; a slight smile turned up the corner of his lips when he recognized her. "Well, Miss Sassy," he said, in a thin, weak voice, "what brings you here?"

Encouraged, Sara moved closer to the bed. "I've come to see how you are feeling, Philip. Does your ankle pain you? Is there anything I can do for you?"

"No, Sara, there is nothing."

"Shall I fetch anything for you?"

"No."

"Would you like your breakfast when Jim Cotton brings it?"

"I—I don't think I can eat this morning, Sara."

She paused a moment, unsure how to go on. There was something about his behavior that alarmed her. In his expression, she saw signs of disappointment mingled with the telltale lines of pain. His tone, when he had spoken, was, she thought, a little fragile and terribly saddened. She realized that from the moment he had first opened his eyes and recognized her, he hadn't once looked at her again.

Instinct told her that something was terribly wrong, and she rushed to the bed, blurting, "Oh, Philip, I have been so worried about you!"

At last he looked up at her with a rather wan smile on his lips. "Have you? You shouldn't, you know. I'll tell you what; if you're very careful and you don't hop about and send a fellow bouncing, you may sit here beside me on the edge of the bed."

"You must be in dreadful pain," she murmured as she gingerly sat down and examined his face anew. "Does your leg trouble you very badly?"

"A little. It's my head more like."

"Your head? But Mr. Deverill said—oh, I knew it! I *knew* the doctor hadn't examined you properly! I should have been on hand to speak to the doctor last night when he came, but Mr. Deverill said I should leave it to him! I dare say you must have struck your head when you fell, Philip. We shall have the doctor back in to examine you for it."

"No. No, it isn't necessary."

"But, Philip, a head injury can be quite serious, I believe. It shall take only a moment to summon the doctor again and—"

"No, Sara," said Philip, much more firmly. "I didn't injure my head in the fall. I never injured it at all. I—oh, God, you shall hate me when I tell you!"

"Hate you? Why on earth should I hate you?"

"Because of what I've done!"

"Philip, you are not making any sense. I'm convinced the doctor must be sent for," said Sara, in deep alarm.

He reached over to clasp her hand in a compelling grip. "Would you just be quiet a moment and listen to what I'm trying to tell you? Aside from a few cuts and bruises, the only thing I injured in the fall was my ankle. Nothing more!"

"Then why does your head hurt so?"

"Because I—! Well, I—! Because when a person drinks too much wine or spirits—no matter how jolly it may make a person feel at the time!—one is made to feel quite wretched the day after." He cast her a probing look. "Do you understand?"

"Yes, I think so. You said last night you were drunk."

"Was I ever! And today I am paying for it, I can assure you! But that's not the worst of it. Sara, I—I have a confession to make to you and—and to tell the truth, I don't know how I shall ever get through it."

"Almost you frighten me!" exclaimed Sara with a slight, nervous laugh of alarm. "What, pray, could you have possibly done that should require a confession?"

"I've behaved the fool, that's what," said Philip, wretchedly. "I never stopped to think, never considered where my actions would lead us, and now it's too late." He paused a moment, summoning his courage, then he looked her in the eye and said, fervently, "Sara, everything's gone! Everything! All our money, Carvington Hall—everything!"

For a moment, she could do little more than stare at him. "What do you mean? What are you saying?" she asked at last.

"Sara, I never meant for this to happen. After I succeeded our father, I started out innocently enough, but once I got to London and set myself up in the town house, everything started to change. I met Hetherington and he introduced me to Deverill and his friends and they were all such high flyers! Very well heeled! I guess I never stopped to think how much money I was spending just to keep up with them. And when Deverill took me to the Nonesuch Club—very exclusive, I can tell you!—I suppose my fate was sealed. By then I had lost a good deal of money gambling, yet I felt I had no choice but to continue on at the faro table, hoping my luck would change. Otherwise, I would have had no way of getting it back, you see. I always thought that if the cards would only turn my way, just once—'' He stopped short, and ran a nervous hand through his hair. After a silent moment he said, in a voice of deep contrition, ''You have every right to hate me!''

Sara was a little stunned by his confession, but at this she said, quite calmly, ''Nonsense! I am sure the situation is not as black as you have painted it.''

''There's more. You might as well know the whole of it! You see, I started selling things off and buying on tick. I left vouchers all over London. When Deverill announced last month that he would follow the Prince to Brighton and would introduce me if I came along, I—I—oh, God, I cannot tell you!''

The anguished note in Philip's voice worked very powerfully on Sara. She asked, breathlessly, ''What is it? What have you done, Philip?''

With considerable difficulty he said, ''I—I mortgaged Carvington Hall to raise the blunt I needed for the trip.''

''You did *what?*'' breathed Sara.

''I can't pay it back,'' he said in utter misery. ''I can't even raise the interest. You would have thought that I might have learned my lesson then, but I didn't. I kept on gambling to try to raise funds—and continued to lose! In the last weeks I've scattered vouchers all over Bath and the worst of it is that I think Deverill has bought them all up.''

''But—but why would he do such a thing?''

''Lord, I don't know! But I dare say if he hadn't, none of the shops would have sold to you, no matter how much money you had put down on account!''

A full minute elapsed before Sara could find her voice. She looked at Philip and found that he was watching her, a wary, probing light in his eyes, as if he were alert to her reaction and had braced himself against it.

Truly, she had no notion what, if anything, to say; her

emotions were in an uproar and alternated between a strong desire to box her brother's ears and an inclination to break down into a fit of crying.

The pressure of her brother's fingers closing over hers should have been reassuring, but instead, Sara found that she could not bring herself to look at him and she turned her head away.

Philip said, quite mournfully, "Truly, Sara, I am sorry I've been such a clunk. I—I wouldn't blame you if you hated me, and there's the truth."

She had never been able to maintain her anger for very long where her brother was concerned. Besides, she decided, boxing his ears would not solve any of their troubles. She shook her head slightly and cast him a look of soft affection. "Oh, Philip, I could never hate you."

"You're a good sister—as good as ever twanged! I'll make it up to you, God as my witness. But the deuce of it is that I have no way of raising any funds, not with this ankle as it is. If I could just get to a card table, I might be in the way of winning some money—even a few shillings would put food on the table, at least!—but now I can't even do that!" He looked at her then, with an expression of great sorrow. "Sara, I—I'm dashed sorry! Truly, I am, but I don't see what's to be done about it all."

"There is nothing for you to do with your ankle as it is," she said. "But there might, perhaps, be something I can do to get us out of this ghastly situation. You must let me handle this, Philip."

"You? How can you handle anything? Sara, a debt is an affair of honor between men! I won't have you meddling!"

"I don't intend to meddle," she retorted firmly. "But neither will I sit idly by and allow Mr. Deverill to take our home out from beneath us, Philip!"

"Really? What will you do?"

"I don't know. But I do know you must only do as I tell

you, from this moment on. Philip, if I ever find you near
a gaming table again, I—I shall kick you!''

He meant to argue with her; he meant to remind her,
in no uncertain terms, who was master of Carvington Hall
and all its domain, but one look into her blue eyes gone
shadowed with trouble and worry, and the words died away
on his lips. His expression softened. He reached over to
lightly cuff her cheek and said, weakly, "If you aren't the
bossiest bit of baggage I ever met."

To hear herself addressed with such fraternal affection
was the most heartening speech Sara had received from
her brother in days. She smiled mistily back at him. "And
you are the most infuriating young man!" She carefully
leaned over and placed a light kiss on his forehead and
was pleased to see him smile in return. "No more fretting
now, if you please! The first thing we must do is have you
rest so your ankle may heal and you must promise to
remain in bed until the doctor allows you to leave it. Promise, now!''

" 'Pon my honor," said Philip, obediently.

She smiled then. "I'll just go see what is keeping Jim
Cotton with your breakfast."

With this cheery note she left the room, closing the door
behind her. But no sooner did she begin to make her way
down the corridor toward the stairs, than her smile faded
and a deep frown of worry marred her brow. Philip's confession had shocked her deeply and she was at a loss to
know what on earth she should do. Unbidden, the thought
came to her to appeal to Hugh, to ask his advice, but when
she chanced to think that Hugh Deverill was very near to
being the cause of their troubles in the first place, that
notion went quickly by the wayside.

She descended the stairs and gained the landing at the
very moment that Hugh, who was climbing the stairs,

reached the very same step. At the sight of her, a spark lit in his grey eyes and he made a slight move toward her.

Instinctively, she stiffened. He was the very last person she could have wished to see at that very moment, but he was standing between her and the steps leading down to the next floor. Short of turning and running in the opposite direction, she had no other choice but to face him.

"Good morning, Sara."

"Good morning, sir," she responded, in a voice so even, she surprised herself.

She made an attempt to pass him, to continue on down the stairs, but his hand on her arm stalled her. Looking up, she saw that he was smiling slightly and that his brow was cocked in a questioning manner. She thought she saw a light of humor in his handsome grey eyes and her chin went up a notch.

"How is our patient this morning, Sara?"

"He is well, sir," she responded in a tight little voice that she hoped would discourage him. "I am on my way to fetch his breakfast. Please excuse me!"

She again made a move to push past him, but his hand remained on her arm and, if anything, his grip there tightened slightly.

"Let Lambert or Jim Cotton take care of such things. They are here to assist you in caring for Carville in any way they can."

"Thank you, I prefer to care for him myself!"

"Sara, there is no shame in accepting help from a friend. Allow me to do this for you; let me put Lambert and Jim Cotton and even myself at your disposal. We're here to help you—even if that help comes only in the form of fetching and carrying for the invalid!"

Sara recognized in his voice a note of low seduction; the same tone he had used on every occasion in which he had succeeded in bending her to his will. The carriage ride, their encounter in the stables—in every instance in which they had been alone together, Hugh Deverill had managed to make her do or say the very thing she knew she shouldn't have done.

And now he was doing it again. In his low, seductive words of concern he had for a moment made her forget the truth—that he and he alone was the chief cause of the predicament in which Sara and Philip now found themselves.

She looked up at him then, the light of battle in her blue eyes, and she asked, coldly, "Haven't you already done enough?"

Hugh's grey eyes widened slightly, then his brows came together and he cast her such a dark look that Sara could hardly guess what he meant to do next.

He showed her in an instant. With a firm grip on her arm, Hugh propelled her toward the nearest door. It opened into the gallery and he ushered her rather ruthlessly across its threshold and into the long, expansive room. Instantly did Sara recall the last time they had been alone together in that very room. Then, he had held her tenderly, seductively; this time, however, his grip upon her arm was as solid and unforgiving as steel.

Hugh closed the door and watched her a moment, then said, still frowning, "I know you'll forgive my curiosity if I ask what the devil you meant by that."

"I meant," said Sara, her back quite rigid, "that your interference is no longer necessary nor welcomed."

"Is that so? Perhaps you had best be plain with me, madam. Are you blaming me for what happened to Carville yesterday?"

"Yes! Yes, I am! And I blame you for a great many other things besides!"

He studied her a moment; her blues were sparking with anger and her slim form was drawn up into a pose of rigid disapproval. That she was agitated there could be no doubt. He said calmly, "I do not think you can have considered what you are saying."

"No? Are you aware or are you not that my—that Lord Carville is on the verge of finding himself penniless?"

"His financial situation is not as bad as—"

"Then you *do* know about his finances!" she interrupted hotly.

"Carville has never confided anything to me of his pecuniary affairs!"

"Must he confide to you what is plain to be seen? You know very well he hasn't the money to keep pace with you and your pursuits of pleasure, yet you allow him to tag after you! You take him to gaming clubs that would never have granted him entrance were it not for you, and then you are so callous as to watch him stand at the gaming tables and lose again and again—and you do *nothing!*"

"Carville is a grown man, capable of making his own decisions! What is it you would have me do, Sara—pluck the cards from his hands?"

"You certainly haven't done anything to discourage him, have you?" she demanded in a tone of strong censure.

"But I didn't *en*courage him, either!"

"Didn't you? You didn't put the bottle of spirits in his hands yesterday, I suppose!"

Hugh flushed angrily. "I offered him a drink! You could hardly hold me to blame!"

"And you merely stood by and watched him drink one glass and then another, and then another! And, when anyone with a particle of sense could see that he was quite beyond the realm of sober thought, you sat by and watched him climb up on that beastly horse of his and gallop off!"

Sara's angry speech, once uttered, hung in the air between them, faintly echoing off the walls of the long gallery. Hugh said nothing; he offered no words of defense nor did he make any gesture of repentance. A dull color crept across his cheeks and a harsh light of anger glittered within the depths of his eyes. Slowly, he relaxed his grip on her arm, then his strong hand fell away completely.

In vain did Sara wait for him to say something, *any*thing, that would refute the accusations she had flung at him. He said nothing. He merely stood by the door, regarding her with an expression mixed of anger and wary assessment. Unless he said something soon, she would have no choice to but believe the worst in him. If he needed encouragement, she was more than willing to offer it to him.

She said, with all the loftiness of one who knew herself to be right, "I see you do not defend yourself! You do not defend yourself because you cannot!"

Hugh's lips went tight with anger. "You have made it clear your opinion of me is already formed."

"Yes! Yes, it is!" she replied, her voice far from steady. "My opinion is that you are a horrid and evil man who preys upon unsuspecting men and—and *bleeds innocents!* I believe those were your very words, were they not?"

Holding himself in rigid check, he said, "Yes, Sara. Those were indeed my very words."

Again did she wait for him to defend himself. Again was she disappointed. She had, she thought, no choice but to believe she was right to maintain a poor and censorious opinion of him. It was a hard lesson to learn that the man she loved was nothing but a gamester, and a rather ruthless one, at that. What's more, he exhibited not the least sign of a man who returned her regard or he wouldn't be content to remain standing not three feet away from her in the most unyielding of poses. Had he held the least affection for her, she reasoned, he would by now have wrapped his strong arms about her and assured her that all her troubles and worries over finances, injured ankles, and gaming vowels would come to naught.

He did none of those things. Instead, Hugh moved toward the door and, with his hand on the knob, looked back at her. "If there is anything you need, you have only to command me."

Hugh left the room before his anger got the better of him; before he lost his temper and educated Sara about the sort of man her brother was; before he lost his self-control and pulled her into his arms and kissed her until she changed her opinion of him.

Luckily, he was able to control himself and his temper; he was not, however, entirely convinced he was better off for it.

It had never occurred to him that Sara might hold him responsible for the behavior of that rascal of a brother of hers, but now it was obvious to him that she did just so. That realization left him feeling quite furious.

He took to the stairs two at a time and threw open the door to his own bedchamber with an unnecessary force.

Lambert, who had but a moment before settled most comfortably in the room's coziest chair, jerked to his feet and was so alarmed by his master's violent entrance, he dropped the freshly laundered neckcloths he had been sorting.

Hugh closed the door with a decided slam. "Don't you scold me, too, Lambert," he recommended, threateningly, "for I won't take it kindly, I assure you!"

Since he had by this time judged that his master's anger stemmed from some source other than entering his room to surprise his valet in the forbidden comfort of his reading chair, Lambert relaxed noticeably. He gathered up the fallen cravats, saying, "I don't usually go about presuming to scold you, sir. But then, you don't usually go about throwing doors off their hinges, either. You've been set off good and proper and I dare say I could guess by whom.''

That bit of presumption stirred the coals of Hugh's anger. "Could you? Could you, now? Damn your impudence, Lambert!''

"As you say, sir, but damning me doesn't change the fact that someone has put a devil among your tailors and I know very well it was the young lord.''

"Well, you're wrong, Lambert. It wasn't Carville who angered me—it was his sister!''

This revelation hung in the air between them; then, without a word, Lambert returned his attention to the neckclothes and quietly resumed his task of folding them.

Hugh watched him in silence for a moment, then he said, pointedly, "I see you aren't shocked or surprised, and you do not protest. That could only mean that you knew, too—you knew that young lady wasn't simply a housekeeper!''

"Begging your pardon, sir, but you didn't truly think you were the only one born with eyes in your head, now, did you?''

Hugh ran a distracted hand through his hair, and laughed unsteadily. "Oh, I have eyes in my head, thank you! Eyes to see a girl who is too outspoken by half! Eyes to see a girl who is pure innocence one moment and pert and willful the next! A girl who has the power to drive me to the brink of—! Lambert, she actually blames me for her brother's injury! She truly believes I alone am responsible for their present circumstance!''

"She couldn't have said so, sir," protested Lambert.

"She did—and more! She looks upon me as some kind of agent of evil sent to earth for the sole purpose of proselytizing the innocent!''

"She's very young," said Lambert, reasonably. "She'll

come about when she's had some time to think on it a bit. In her heart, I'm sure madam knows what sort of man her brother is, but she's not yet ready to admit it, even to herself.''

Hugh sat down on the edge of the bed. He propped his elbows on his knees and wearily rubbed his fingers over his eyes. "Perhaps she is not far from wrong about me," he said, after a moment. "Perhaps she is not wrong at all."

"Perhaps," said his valet, wisely avoiding a commitment to either camp.

"The devil of it is, that I think she has gauged me more accurately than I care to admit. You know, I never considered it before, but—damme, what if she is right? What if I *am* responsible for what happened to Carville yesterday?''

"*You*, sir? I don't see as how that may be!"

"I'll tell you how: I introduced him to a social circle that was well beyond his financial means. Oh, I didn't know it at the time, but when I did discover it, I did nothing to dissuade him. Were it not for me, Carville never would have gained entree into a gaming world where high stakes were the norm and the sight of a man losing a fortune in a single sitting was uneventful—perhaps, even commonplace."

Lambert shook his head. "You could have no notion how badly dipped his lordship was."

"Didn't I? I certainly knew it last week, in the tailor's shop, when Carville tried to purchase that God-awful waistcoat on credit that was swiftly denied. I knew then just how badly the lad's pockets were to let."

"Yes, and once you did know, you took steps to keep his lordship away from the gaming tables!"

Hugh looked up at him sharply. "Did I?"

"Yes, you did; and you used some very odd pretexts, in my opinion: an evening at the theater, a promise to play billiards, a visit to the assembly rooms—perhaps madam is too young and innocent of your ways to know when you're disporting yourself in places that are not at all in your line, but *I* am not so easily fooled!''

"If you had possessed any better ideas for keeping the lad from the gaming tables, I wish you would have told me.''

"I suppose neither one of us is at all used to planning entertainments that don't involve one form of vice or another,'' said Lambert with a smile. "I dare say that's the reason you could think of nothing more than getting the young lord drunk in order to keep him at home.''

"Does nothing escape your notice?'' asked Hugh with a frown that Lambert knew from experience was more a sign of discouragement than anger.

"Rarely, sir!'' grinned Lambert.

Hugh stood and took a rather agitated turn about the room, which ended by the window that looked out across the east lawn. He stared thoughtfully at the view a moment. "Then it's true. I *am* responsible. I could have used some other means to keep him from gambling yesterday, but I didn't. Instead, I encouraged him to drink—one glass after another all afternoon!—until he could barely weave a path to the stables. Sara was right: I *did* get the foolish puppy drunk. I *am* responsible for his injury!''

"He'll heal,'' said Lambert, philosophically. He cast a pointed look at his employer and added, "As will the young lady's heart.''

That brought Hugh's head round with a snap. "Damn your impudence, Lambert!''

"As you say, sir,'' murmured his valet, unperturbed.

"The young lady happens to consider me no better than the devil incarnate!''

"Yes, sir. But I rather think if that were so, the young lady would have taken steps to have you put from the house.''

"She has! Several times, as a matter of fact."

Lambert shook his head. "No, sir. She has applied only to the young lord on the matter, knowing full well that his will is less than strong where you are concerned, if you'll forgive my saying."

"But aside from her brother, who else would she apply to?"

"If she truly wanted you put from the house, she would have appealed to Lord Westbury for assistance," said Lambert, revealing a knowledge of the intimacies of the lives of his betters he had hitherto concealed.

Hugh turned his attention back to the vista outside his window and after a quiet moment, said, "I think you may be right, Lambert."

"As you say, sir."

"I also think it may be time I paid a call on Westbury. Have Jim saddle my horse, will you? I'll ride into town instead of taking the curricle so Jim may remain behind to wait upon the invalid."

"Yes, sir."

"I suppose if I am to be held responsible for creating this ghastly mess, I must be held responsible for doing what I can to fix it."

"As you say, sir. What shall I tell madam when she asks after you?"

"What makes you think she shall ask after me?"

Lambert's only response was to fix his master with a pointed look from beneath raised eyebrows.

"Damn your impudence, Lambert!"

Chapter Thirteen

It wasn't long after Hugh finished consigning his valet's soul to the netherworld that he rode into Bath on a direct course for Lord Westbury's house. He was ushered into the front hall just as Westbury himself was descending the stairs, his hat and gloves in his hand.

His lordship pulled up short at the sight of him, saying, "Deverill! What the deuce?"

"I've come to speak with you on a matter of some importance, Westbury. Spare me a moment, will you?"

"I was just leaving the house, frankly. I'm engaged to escort my mother to the Pump Room. Can it wait?"

"No, it can't," replied Hugh with an unnerving gaze.

His lordship hesitated a moment, then said, "Very well. But I can give you only a moment, mind!"

He ushered Hugh into a small sitting room just off the hall and set his gloves and hat down on a table. "What is it you want, Deverill?"

Hugh's dark brow flew skyward. "You're being direct!"

"I see no reason to beat a path about a bush and waste good manners between us. You don't like me any more than I like you, after all is said."

"True. But for all our differences, we do have one thing in common, I think."

Lord Westbury fixed him with a hard glare. "We have *nothing* in common!"

"You mistake. Or perhaps you have not considered your affection for Carville and his sister. Especially his sister."

"Have a care how you proceed, Deverill," warned Lord Westbury. "You'll understand, I know, that I dislike hearing Miss Brandon-Howe's name on the lips of a man of your reputation."

"And that is precisely the reason I am here," said Hugh, amiably. Unbidden, he sat down on a settee and settled himself comfortably, crossing one ankle over his knee. "I rather wonder that you never took steps to warn either Carville or Miss Brandon-Howe off me."

"Don't flatter yourself, Deverill. I did warn them, especially Miss Brandon-Howe. I told her on more than one occasion exactly what sort of man you are."

"And . . ."

"And . . . she wouldn't listen to me."

"Take heart. I have a notion she'll listen to you now. And this time, I would be grateful if you would follow your revelations about my character with an invitation to stay with you and your mother here in town."

That request surprised Lord Westbury. "Ask her to stay? Here, in Bath, with my family?"

"That's what I said, Westbury. Well, are you willing to invite her to stay with you or are you not?"

"Well, of course, I am willing! But she will never go. She will never leave her brother," said his lordship. "And that's the pity of it. In my heart, I believe I have a great degree of affection for Carville as I have for Miss Brandon-

Howe, but he does try me, at times. He's a rascal, when all is said and done, but his sister is devoted to him."

"I know all about Carville and the sort of lad he is. I dare say there's no real vice in him, but he does have a lot to learn about life—including a long lesson on caring for the reputations of the females in his family."

Lord Westbury favored him with a hard frown. "I am well aware that Carville has allowed his sister to remain in the house, unchaperoned, with two other bachelors in residence. It's an unusual situation, but as long as her brother is in a position to protect her, neither the lady nor her reputation are in any real danger."

"But it still bothers you, doesn't it?"

"Of course it does! A young lady must guard herself against the *appearance* of impropriety just as much as the impropriety itself! I assure you, the entire town is acquainted with Miss Brandon-Howe's situation at Carvington Hall. I do my best to protect against the rumors, but I can only do so much!"

"You're going to have to do more," said Hugh, "because the situation at Carvington Hall has changed. Carville has met with a small accident."

"Good lord! Has he—"

"A minor injury, nothing serious, I assure you! But he is confined to his bed for a few days and when he does at last get himself up and about, he'll be hobbling between two sticks." He graciously allowed Lord Westbury a few moments to digest this information. "I dare say at this moment Carville wouldn't know what his sister was up to if she were in the next room, to say nothing of preventing her from committing some folly against her reputation. Plainly spoke, Carville is in no position to protect his sister or her good name."

"Good God," uttered his lordship, as he mentally examined the possibilities. "When news of this gets about the neighborhood, her reputation will be ... she'll never recover!''

"That is her fate, I fear, unless she is removed from the house immediately and stays away until her brother is back on his feet."

"Young Carville must be made to see the sense of it!"

"You let me take care of Carville; I want you to concentrate on Miss Brandon-Howe. Now, give me your word, Westbury! Say you will drive out to Carvington Hall and fetch her to stay with you!"

"Yes! Yes, I shall!" proclaimed Lord Westbury, roused to heroism.

"Good. And don't keep me waiting. I want her out of that house without delay!"

Lord Westbury cast him an odd look. "Do you? I would have guessed a man of your excesses would have been only too willing to take advantage of her predicament."

"You do have a poor opinion of me, don't you?" asked Hugh, but in such a pleasant tone that his lordship was not the least intimidated.

"Bluntly, yes, I do! So I know you'll forgive my asking why your behavior is so completely out of order. Your reputation where women is concerned is well known and probably quite deserved, and yet you are making every effort to protect the reputation of a young, attractive girl you have spent the better part of two weeks with. Why, it's almost as if you had developed a sudden regard for the proprieties and—'' He stopped short, as an expression of dawning recognition crossed his face. He said, in a wondrous tone, "You're—you're in love with her!"

"You're talking through your hat, Westbury," said Hugh, flicking his lordship a look of annoyance.

"Am I? *Am* I? I would disagree with you. I would disagree with you most heartily!" He waited for Hugh to offer some sort of protest. When he realized it was not forthcoming, his lordship smiled a bit triumphantly. "So! Devil Deverill has been brought to his knees at last! The great *roué* has fallen in love!"

"Leave it to you to kick up a dust cloud around nothing! You're speaking nonsense, Westbury."

"I think not! I think you have a tenderness for the girl. Yet, for the sake of her well-being, you are willing to throw her into my path when you have observed very well that my attentions toward Miss Brandon-Howe have been constant! I never knew you for a chivalrous man, Deverill!"

"You don't know me at all," retorted Hugh, at last succumbing to impatience, "and you're confusing chivalry with common sense. I simply want you to remove the girl from Carvington Hall so as not to incite rumor."

"You mean, remove Miss Brandon-Howe so as not to incite *you!*" interpolated Lord Westbury with a faint smile of amusement.

Hugh rose slowly and deliberately to his feet, prompting his lordship to say, quickly, "I am sure you would like to hit me, but I'm equally sure you will not. You cannot strike a man for speaking the truth, Deverill!"

"You're speaking nothing but rubbish!"

"I could spend the rest of the day disagreeing with you, but to what point? As long as you are not ready to acknowledge your feelings for Miss Brandon-Howe, I gain an advantage! Very well, Deverill! I shall call at Carvington Hall and whisk her back here to my home in Bath. And while she is a guest in my home, I intend to do everything in my power to fix her affections on me!"

"Do as you wish, Westbury. I assure you, I have no intentions—honorable or otherwise—toward Miss Sara Brandon-Howe!"

No sooner did Hugh utter those words, than he knew them to be false. He did have intentions toward Sara; intentions that, left to his own devises, he might never have recognized or examined on his own. Westbury's accusations forced him to confront his own emotions, and he returned to Carvington Hall feeling a trifle off-balance, somewhat bemused, and decidedly unsure of his own mind. Until he had received in stunned silence Westbury's smug analysis of his character, Hugh had never before examined the reasons for his own behavior nor had he ever stopped to contemplate the emotions that drove him to act as he did.

But now that he considered it, he realized that his conduct was certainly out of the normal way. Feminine affection had never been something he had made a habit of cultivating. In his experience, females had a tendency to mistake a passing conversation for companionship, and companionship for some more permanent relation. For a man of his avocation, nothing could be more disastrous than to find himself leg-shackled to a wife; a wife who would demand from him cozy evenings by the fire, when he would as lief spend his nights holding the bank at a faro table.

He had spent his last three and thirty years avoiding just such a situation, taking whatever steps necessary to prevent any feminine influence encroaching on his life. Only two short weeks ago he would have had no more intention of involving himself in the affairs of a slip of a girl such as Sara Brandon-Howe, than he would have considered throwing himself into the Thames. But something about her had changed all that.

She intrigued him as much as she entertained him; her guilelessness was as touching to him as was her unfailing devotion to her brother. She conjured in him feelings he had not known he possessed; feelings of loyalty and companionship and an overwhelming desire to play the role of the gallant *chevalier* and shield her from the folly of her own actions.

Without realizing, he had found himself seeking her out, using every pretext and ploy in his repertoire to gain and retain her attentions. Even more surprising was that he demanded from her nothing in return. Instead, he had his reward in the fleeting glimpse of her reluctant smile; in seeing her blue eyes shine with gratitude whenever he chanced to please her; or in the memory of their afternoon in the stables when she had stood so compliantly before him, awaiting the touch of his lips against hers.

For the first time did he realize that in slow but steady degrees it had become a matter of importance that she trust him, that she confide to him the reason that would cause her to masquerade as a servant in her own household. That her brother was behind the plot, there could be no doubt; that Hugh wanted Sara to trust him and allow him to extricate her from the ridiculous situation in which her brother had placed her was an even stronger truth. But until she trusted him, until she confided her predicament to him, he was powerless to change her circumstance.

It was rather beyond his ability to admit to himself why, indeed, he coveted Sara's trust or even why he wished to influence her life. Even more was he at a loss to understand the attraction he felt for such a managing, opinionated young woman who was, in truth, little more than a school-girl. She was young and she was innocent. To a man like Hugh Deverill who usually liked his women to sport a certain air of experience, those qualities made Sara as dangerous to him as she was attractive. He was rather convinced that the next time he put his fingers beneath her chin, he would not be able to summon a gentlemanly resolve and merely brush her lips. The next time he found himself close to her, he wouldn't be able to resist holding her and, at the very least, kissing her full, sweet lips. At the most, he could very well plot her seduction.

Luckily, he would not be called upon to summon such

inner strength. If Westbury kept his promise—and Hugh had no doubt that he would, since the man was a veritable pattern card of honesty—Sara would very soon be whisked away to the safety of Westbury's house in Bath.

Until Westbury called to collect her, it only remained for Hugh to avoid Sara's presence so he would not be tempted to throw his gentleman's resolve right out the nearest window.

Chapter Fourteen

Sara discovered the hard way that Philip was just as unruly a patient as he was inattentive as a brother. He disliked being left alone in his room and by the afternoon following his fall, he had begun to complain bitterly of boredom. His foot, he told Sara fretfully, caused him awful pain and he made it known that it was his opinion that the doctor had conspired against him by not leaving a sufficient dose of sleeping powders that would put him well to sleep so he would not feel any pain at all.

Lambert and Jim Cotton offered to take turns staying with Philip so Sara might go about her duties. As grateful as she might have been at such a show of kindness, she considered that any assistance she might accept from Lambert and Jim was, by extension, assistance from Hugh Deverill. She was determined not to be beholden to the man and declined the kind offer the men had made.

Late that afternoon, Philip fell into a fitful but merciful sleep and Sara wearily curled up in a chair by the window with a book of poetry. A soft scratch at the door announced Lambert. He entered the room with the intelligence that Lord Westbury had called and had been ushered into the drawing room.

"His lordship is very anxious to see you, madam, and I have been charged to send you to him," whispered Lambert. "Never you fear; I'll stay with Lord Carville and tend him if he should wake."

Grateful, Sara thanked him very prettily and went downstairs to find Lord Westbury waiting for her.

He went to her as soon as she entered the room, and clasped both her hands in his. "Sara! I came as soon as I heard of your situation. How is your brother? His injuries are not serious, I am told."

"Not at all, thankfully," she answered, "but his ankle pains him and has made him cross, I think. I should advise you not to visit him until he can speak more sociably!"

"I understand. I understand, too, that your good humor does you credit. Philip is lucky to have a sister such as you."

"Believe me, I have done nothing to earn such praise," protested Sara, laughing slightly. "I merely sit beside him and try to divert his attention from his injury. I have no other responsibilities for his care or for his comfort."

"That I cannot believe!"

"It is true, I assure you. At the risk of losing your good opinion, I must tell you that Mr. Deverill's valet and tiger have the care of Philip. I, on the other hand, am quite useless!"

"Then it would not be a hardship on your brother if I were to whisk you away for a short while."

Sara blinked at him in surprise. "Whisk me away? Pray, what do you mean, Lord Westbury?"

"I am asking you to reconsider my offer. I am asking

you to come to Bath for a while, to stay with my mother and me.''

"I don't understand," she said, in deep confusion. "Didn't you already invite me to do so? And didn't I already refuse that invitation, with the greatest thanks?''

"You did. But, Sara, I fear your circumstances have changed.''

"Have they? I don't see how.''

"Then allow me to explain it to you. You see, your circumstances were altered the moment your brother became unable to protect you.''

She gave a light, forced laugh. "Protect me? Protect me from what?''

"From Hugh Deverill, of course!''

"I assure you, Lord Westbury, that Mr. Deverill poses not the least threat to me! Why, on the contrary, he has been a perfect gentleman where I am concerned. Why, I should rely upon him for protection from outsiders, that's how greatly I hold him in esteem!''

His lordship frowned. "Sara, I think you are making a grave mistake. I think you would do better to come home with me, and allow my mother to guide you a little.''

"But my home is here, at Carvington Hall. My lord, I know you mean well, and I thank you for your concern, but I will not leave my brother, and I assure you, Mr. Deverill poses no threat to me or my virtue.''

Clearly, Lord Westbury did not care for Sara's decision, but seemed to realize that, short of picking her up and physically hoisting her into his carriage, she was not going to leave Carvington Hall. He left her, a bit reluctantly, she thought, and she was able at last to return to Philip's room.

There she found Lambert standing sentinel outside the door, and most unwilling to give up his post. "I'll stay with him a little more, madam. Perhaps you should like to take your supper before you come back to sit with him.''

"Lambert, it is very kind of you to wish to help, but it is not at all necessary, you know."

"That may be as that may be, but I shall remain here, all the same, madam."

Short of engaging in a rather undignified shoving match with the man, Sara could not hit upon any plan for gaining entry into her brother's room and sending Lambert on his way.

She did, however, secure a promise from Lambert that he would call her if her brother awoke and, realizing that she would have to be satisfied with that small assurance, she reluctantly went away. Evening came and Sara returned with the full intention of nursing her brother, but this time she found Lambert gone and Jim Cotton ruling the sickroom. He, too, proved unwilling to brook any suggestion that he give up his post.

For the first time in nearly two days Sara found herself with nothing to do; no duties pressed upon her, no brother commanded her to fetch and carry. She retreated to the quiet of her room and remained there until well into the evening, when Daisy arrived, bearing a tray filled with supper dishes.

"I didn't suspect you would be down for dinner, so I took the liberty, miss," she said, as she drew a small table near Sara's chair and arranged the plates upon it. "Properly hungered you should be, too, what with not having a thing to eat since a few slices of toast at breakfast."

The gentle aroma of food caught Sara's attention. "Do you know, I believe I am very hungry, Daisy! Thank you!"

"Then you'll be eating everything on your plate!" she answered, with a stern look as if she thought she might meet with an argument. "I'll be back to clear away a bit later. Can I get anything else for you, miss?"

"No, nothing, I think. I mean to spend the next few hours here in my room, enjoying the solitude."

"I've the very thing for you, then: a nice hot bath! There's nothing more relaxing, if that's what you've a mind for. I could have the water brought up for you, miss, and I dare say though I've never been a lady's maid, I might be able to lend a hand in washing and brushing your hair just like a true abigail would."

Sara was clearly tempted. "If it's not too much trouble . . ."

"None at all!" said Daisy, with a smile. "Leave everything to me!"

In Daisy's very capable hands did Sara pass the rest of the evening. By midnight she was quite alone, having sent Daisy to her own bed. She was feeling very warm and comforted as she sat before the fire, drying her hair in front of the flames.

She had just made up her mind to retire to her bed when she heard a light rap on her door.

"Who is there?" she called.

"It's only me, madam—Jim Cotton!"

She opened the door a crack and peered at him. "Yes, Jim, what is it?"

"It's the young lord, madam. He woke up a bit ago and has gone very fretful and won't rest easy no matter what Lambert or I think to do for him. He's asked for you, madam. Will you come?"

"Of course! Tell Lord Carville I shall be with him directly, only I must get dressed first."

"Oh, madam, you'd best come now. Don't worry as to how you are dressed; Lambert and I shall excuse ourselves until the young lord does fall asleep or until you ring us to come back."

"Go back to Lord Carville, then. I shall be with you presently."

She closed the door and went to her wardrobe where she drew from its depths a simple wrapper of blue silk, which she donned over her nightdress, and a pair of slippers to guard her bare feet against the cold floors.

In Philip's room she found both Lambert and Jim Cotton hovering about her brother's bed. They discreetly left the room as soon as she entered, assuring her as they went that they were quite prepared to return to tend the invalid if only she would but ring.

Philip was lying in the center of the massive old bed, looking a trifle wan and decidedly peevish. He turned his head to look at her and said, quite belligerently, "So, it's true! You meant to go off to sleep without so much as a care that I might have been suffering!"

Sara ignored this outburst. "You're causing quite a stir, Philip. What do you mean by it?"

"It's this wretched foot of mine. It hurts me, you know, to such a degree that I think that doctor who examined it must have missed a broken bone. I tell you, I cannot be comfortable!"

"I think you can, if only you could divert your thoughts to something else besides your injury. Shall we play a game together?"

"No!"

"Would you like to send some correspondence? I could write as you dictate."

"Don't be ridiculous! There's no one on this green earth I would lief write to, I assure you!"

"Then perhaps you would like me to read to you. I dare say a good story will take your mind off your foot for a while so you may at last get some rest."

"Very well!" said Philip, with little good grace. "But don't think for a moment I'll sit idly by while you read me one of those prosing epics of yours, for I won't stand for it!"

"No, indeed. If you like, I shall fetch my Anne Radcliffe, which I think you shall like very well. It is full of tales of murderous wives and husbands with dark secrets. It is called *The Mysteries of Udolpho*. I shall fetch it for you.''

Outside Philip's bedroom Sara found Jim Cotton standing guard. "Is there anything I can do, madam? Can I get something for you?"

"No, Jim. I am just going down to the library to fetch a book to read to Lord Carville. I shall be only a moment but perhaps you might be good enough to listen for him, in case he calls out."

The rooms on the lower floors of the house were dark, their candles snuffed long ago as one by one, first Sara then the rest of the household, had prepared for bed. Even in the darkness, Sara needed no candle to light her way; she knew each step, each carpeted stair, each creaking floorboard in the dear old house. She made her way down the stairs to the first floor without mishap.

In the library a low fire still burned in the grate, left unattended to die down of its own accord. In the dim light of the dying embers, Sara struggled to find *The Mysteries of Udolpho* among the many volumes on the shelves that lined the walls of the room. She had just made up her mind to light a candle to cast some light upon her search when a sound behind her caused her to turn quickly.

In the darkness she saw a light spark to life and in the halo of the light it cast she realized that Hugh was in the room, sitting in an overstuffed chair drawn before the fire. In his hand was a lighted spill and as she watched, he lit a cigar.

His coat and neckcloth were lying over the top of a nearby table and he was slouched very low in his chair, his long muscled legs stretched out before him. He looked very much the way he had appeared in the stables the day before, and Sara found herself submitting to the same tug of attraction for him that she had felt then.

"I—I thought you were gone!" she said at last in a

breathless voice. "I thought you had gone to town to meet Lord Hetherington."

At first he didn't appear to have heard her; he certainly took his time answering. He puffed at his cigar and said at last, very quietly, "No. No, I did not go into Bath. Even though you don't think me capable of helping care for Carville, I do know you rely upon my tiger. I stayed behind tonight on the chance you might have need of Jim Cotton."

Her eyes at last adjusted to the dim light of the room, Sara spied on the table resting close by Hugh's elbow a tray on which reposed a glass and a near-empty bottle of port. He had consumed quite a bit of wine, if that bottle were anything to judge by, but she didn't think he sounded at all intoxicated. Certainly, his words were clear and not the least slurred; his eyes, still focused on the ebbing light of the flames in the hearth, were still intelligent and keen.

She took a step toward him. "Jim has been very helpful to me, thank you. He—he is with Philip now, as a matter of fact. I—I was just now fetching a book to read. Philip cannot sleep, you see."

"So he dragged you from your sleep to tell you so! Thoughtful of him!"

Her first instinct was to defend Philip, to tell Hugh Deverill in no uncertain terms that he had no right to speak so, but the words died away as quickly as they came to mind. Realizing herself to be little more than a brazen traitor, Sara allowed him to speak so of her brother. She would have allowed him further license, as long as she could remain in his presence.

She brushed aside all the many concerns and criticisms she had entertained about Mr. Deverill. She still abhorred his way of life, she still wished to snap the rein of influence he held over Philip. In her heart she believed that every one of the horrid things she had said to him earlier that day had been true and remarkably justified.

Yet, at the same time, Sara could not deny the fact that no matter how sensible she may be of his shortcomings, she was terribly attracted to Hugh.

Since the moment of their meeting he had shown her a very gentle side to his character that, try as she might, she could not correlate to his worldly reputation. It was that gentleness that had broken down her defenses and made her forget who he was and what he stood for. It was that gentleness that had, she knew, caused her to lose her heart to him. Even now, in the simple surroundings of the book room of a country manor, she found his presence compelling. She knew she should leave; she knew she should not be alone with a man of his reputation, but she found herself instead searching for a reason to stay.

She took a few more tentative steps toward him. "You—you haven't seen, I suppose, my copy of Mrs. Radcliffe's book lying about, have you?"

He looked at her then, for the first time since she had entered the library.

He looked back into the mesmerizing flames dancing in the hearth and muttered, "Go back to your bed, little Sara."

She never considered obeying him. Indeed, she moved closer to him. "Oh, I am not the least tired so I do not need my bed. And I have no reason to hurry back to Philip, for Jim is with him now. He has been very good to help and I—I know he does so because you have told him he must. Thank you!"

A full minute passed in silence. At last Hugh looked at her again, but this time, there was a look of dark intensity in his eyes. "Sara, you should not stay here with me now."

"Why?" she asked, her heart quickening just a bit.

"Because we cannot be alone together. You know my reputation and you know my character. You've certainly thrown them in my face often enough, thanks, no doubt, to Westbury.''

Sara wasn't very well schooled in the subject of men and their behaviors and temperaments, but she knew a jealous tone when she heard one. It gave her courage. ''I pay no heed to Lord Westbury's advice, for I find it merely echoes the very same advice you have already given me.''

He frowned at her. ''What are you talking about?''

''I am talking about the fact that Lord Westbury called upon me this afternoon under the pretext of commiserating over Philip's injury.''

Hugh cocked one dark brow in question. ''Pretext? Did you doubt the man's sincerity?''

''Not at all! But I also know he has been concerned for my safety since the day you first arrived at Carvington Hall. Today he suggested that I should leave the Hall and stay, instead, with him and his mother in Bath.''

''That sounds like an excellent suggestion.''

''Do you think so? I did not, I assure you. I refused his kind offer, you see.''

Hugh looked at her a moment, an odd frown clouding his eyes. ''That was a foolish thing to do, Sara.''

''Why do you say so?''

''Because whatever you think of his invitation, you must know Westbury has only your welfare at heart.''

''I never thought to hear you defend Lord Westbury,'' said Sara. ''I often rather thought you disliked the man.''

''Like, dislike—what does that matter? The man's intentions are well-founded; he's merely concerned for your safety. You would be wise to accept his offer!''

Sara shook her head slightly. ''I think Lord Westbury's concern for my safety centers around you. He fears for my reputation, my virtue, as long as you remain a guest in the house. He is unaware that yesterday you made me a promise that you would not seduce me.''

* * *

That was one promise Hugh was having a devil of a time keeping. She wasn't making it any easier on him by standing so close upon him, gowned in such an alluring manner. He itched to run his palms down the smooth, soft length of her silk dressing gown; what she was wearing beneath the flimsy bit of material his imagination could only guess at. He knew that if he left his chair, if he stood to face her, his resolve would be gone and—promise be damned!—he wouldn't be able to say with any certainty that he could maintain the chivalrous pose he had adopted where Sara Brandon-Howe was concerned.

He knew all those things, yet he discarded them in an instant. He rose to his feet and he was a little unnerved to realize just how close Sara was to him; close enough so that, if he had a mind to, he had only to reach out his hand to touch the soft cloud of her hair as it caught and reflected the dancing lights from the hearth. He was close enough merely to reach out to trail a single finger down the long and slender column of her neck.

She looked up at him and asked softly, "You do still promise, don't you? You still promise you won't behave as any other but a gentleman?"

"If I made that promise, Sara, would you believe me?"

"Yes," she said without hesitation. "I know I was quite wicked this morning and said some horrid things to you. I—I don't know that I believe everything I said. I do know, however, that you are a man of honor and—and if you give me your word, I—I shall believe you, no matter what you may think to the contrary."

He didn't answer her because he wasn't sure what on earth he could say. From the first moment of their acquaintance, she had intrigued him and mesmerized him and called him to actions he barely recognized as his own;

noble and unselfish and honest actions that he hadn't
entertained in years. But he was entertaining them now
He was entertaining them for Sara.

Yes, he had promised he wouldn't seduce her, but he
didn't think there could be much harm in kissing her. A
simple, gentle kiss; nothing more than a light sip from the
sweetness of her lips poised so invitingly close to his. He
was a strong man, a man of will power. What harm could
there be in just a kiss?

Slowly, he bent his head until at last his lips brushed
against hers. It was a gentle kiss, almost teasing, but it was
enough to cause Sara to step instinctively closer. After a
moment, Hugh raised his head.

Sara looked up at him, her blue eyes clouded and softly
focused on the chiseled line of his lips. "Again," she commanded, as greedy as a child after her first taste of mar-
zipan.

Almost he laughed; almost he chided her for being too
eager. But one look into her blue eyes and he instantly
changed his mind. In her eyes he saw a small spark of
passion fan to life and he never doubted for a moment
that his kiss had been the cause of it. He should have
stepped away from her then; he should have resolved to
leave her and the shadowed invitation of the library far
behind, but he didn't.

What ultimately decided his course of action, he could
not say; perhaps it was the provocative manner in which
the thin blue wrapper fell enticingly over the curves of her
body; perhaps it was the manner in which her voice had
gone soft and breathy as she spoke that one, simple word
It didn't matter the cause; the effect was that before he
knew it, before he could consider his actions, he took her
in his arms and kissed her again.

He was a skillful and insistent aggressor; his lips took
masterful possession of hers like an invader, plundering

the sweetness of her mouth, holding her captive with unwavering pressure. Her head fell back against his shoulder and she clung to him, savoring every movement of his lips against hers, of his broad hands across the narrow span of her waist. His fingers plunged amid the waves of golden brown hair that fell down her back, claiming even more of her as his own.

He left her lips for a moment, to trail a string of fiery kisses down her neck and along the smooth line of her chin; then once again did he return his attention to her lips, taking undisputed possession of them, commanding her to his will.

Sara succumbed readily, never considering that she had begun to trod dangerous ground. She knew only that Hugh was kissing her, holding her, reducing her to little more than a feeling of warm, delicious trembles. She resisted nothing and when she felt his hands skim along her waist to where the sash was tied to hold her wrapper in place, she didn't resist. She could think only of the manner in which his fingers seemed to leave a trail of fire wherever they touched.

He loosened the bow without effort and plunged his fingers inside the folds of the wrapper. Only the thin material of her nightgown stood between him and his goal and he wasn't about to let it stop him. He moved his hands to her shoulders and gently slid the wrapper down her arms until it caught at her elbows.

Her nightdress was simple lawn, the material almost sheer, with a narrow wedge of lace about the neck through which a pale blue ribbon had been threaded to hold the garment's fullness in place. He bent his head to kiss a string of fire down her neck, fully intent upon journeying on toward the pale blue bow, the only obstacle that stood between him and the sweetness of his goal.

His lips traveled further and he pressed a kiss into the softness of her shoulder. He heard her gasp with delight, and he obligingly did it again. She murmured softly, and he raised his head for the merest of moments, so he could look down on her.

Her blue eyes were dark and liquid from the intensity of his kisses and her lashes fluttered low over her eyes. Her hands were knotted in the silk fabric of his shirt, clutching at him, holding onto him as if she were half afraid she might sink into a puddle on the floor.

She gave a shuddering sigh. "D—don't stop."

He had long made it a practice to never argue with a lady; he had no intention of starting now. Hugh promptly adjusted his arms about her, enveloping her as securely against him as he could. Then he bent his head once again to claim her lips, his intent once again upon the prize of the thin blue ribbon.

This time, Sara loosened her grip upon his shirt and tentatively, inexpertly, returned his embrace. Her fingers danced lightly against his back, as if she were unsure or shy as to how she should hold him. Hers was the embrace of an innocent, and no sooner did Hugh recognize it as such than he was immediately sobered.

In an instant he recalled the promise he had made to her in the stables, the same promise he had reiterated when first she had come into the room. He had vowed he wouldn't seduce her; he was perilously close to breaking that vow.

His lips left hers and he turned his head slightly away from her. He clenched his eyes shut as he fought against the lure of the pale blue ribbon.

"What—what is it?" asked Sara, in a voice barely above a whisper. "What is wrong?"

He couldn't bring himself to look at her. "Just a minute," he said, sounding slightly strangled and decidedly distant. "I just—I just need a minute."

He didn't let her go, but his hold about her certainly loosened. At last he looked down at her and saw that her cheeks were flushed and her blue eyes had gone wide with doubt and concern. Her full lips were parted slightly to form a delicate, questioning "O." It took every ounce of will he possessed not to claim those lips, to part them further, to plunder them again until his hunger for her was sated.

But he didn't. Instead, he took a deep breath and leaned down to tenderly kiss her forehead. "Go to your bed, little Sara. Go now, before I forget the promise I made you."

With surprisingly steady hands, he drew the wrapper back up over her shoulders, then with a hand at her elbow, he ushered her to the door.

"I—I don't understand," she said uncertainly, as she found herself being propelled out into the hall. "Did—did I do something wrong?"

"No, Sara."

"Did—did I displease you?"

"No, Sara, and therein lies the trouble. I fear you pleased me very much, indeed."

Chapter Fifteen

It was impossible for Sara to return to Philip's room and behave as if nothing out of the ordinary had occurred. Something *had* occurred; something so monumental and extraordinary, she felt certain her life would never again be the same because of it.

Sara had long suspected herself to be a little bit in love with Hugh Deverill; after experiencing the thrill of his kisses in the library, she was now heartily convinced of it. Truly, she wanted nothing more in life than to remain within the circle of his strong embrace, and to feel once again the pressure of his lips on hers. It was, therefore, she thought, a rather curious circumstance to discover that the man who could in one moment reduce her to quaking compliance with several simple kisses, could in the next moment escort her from the room with almost insulting composure.

She wasn't at all sure she understood his behavior, but, then, she knew nothing of the art of love-making. If, indeed, what had passed between them in the library was any indication of the manner in which one did make love, Sara was quite willing to allow that Hugh Deverill could take her in his arms and kiss her senseless any time he had a mind to. Certainly, he would encounter no argument from her.

Wondrously, happily, she relived in her imagination the thrill of Hugh's kisses. Indeed, she was halfway up the stairs to the second floor when she realized she had failed to retrieve the book that had sent her to the library in the first place. Of a sudden did she recall her duty to Philip, alone and fretful in his bed, relying upon her return to ease his discomfort.

Going to him would, she knew, be the right thing to do; soothing Philip's irascible mood would be the act of a loyal and loving sister. But for the second time that evening, she made a traitorous decision.

Sara went straight to her room, knowing full well that she was abandoning her brother for the more fulfilling prospect of reliving in her imagination for just a little while longer the thrill of Hugh's kisses.

It was very late indeed when at last she fell asleep and late, too, the next morning when Daisy woke her by pulling back the heavy draperies to allow in the morning sunlight.

"You must wake up, miss. Lord Carville has been asking for you."

"Has he?" Sara asked, as she indulged in a long and satisfying stretch. "Goodness, I had no idea the hour was so far advanced. I should have slept the day away had you not come in just now!"

"Worn out, you are, and that's the truth. I gave Lord Carville a proper scold on your behalf because of it," said Daisy.

Sara swung her legs over the side of the bed and cast

her a look of mild amusement. "Did you? What did you say to scold my brother?"

" 'Shame on you,' says I, 'for keeping miss up until all hours of the night!' " Daisy mounted one hand on her hip and with her other hand, wagged an admonishing finger in the air. "Says I, 'shame on you for making poor miss weary from lack of sleep!' Well, he didn't say a word back, for what, indeed, could he say? Especially when I told him you were looking fagged to death from all your fetching and carrying for him."

"And my brother let you speak to him that way?" asked Sara, entertained, but doubtful. "He allowed you to address him in just that tone?"

"He couldn't very well quarrel with me, after all, what with Mr. Deverill standing right there by his bed and nodding agreement with everything I said."

At her dressing table, Sara had been about to splash her face with fresh water from the bowl, but at this, she stopped and turned wide eyes toward Daisy. "Mr. Deverill? He was with Philip? And he *agreed* with you?"

"Not in so many words, but I could tell by the way he nodded just so"—Daisy demonstrated a curt little motion—"that he recognized the truth in what I said. For all his stiff shirts, Mr. Deverill is a gentleman, I think, and he is very kind to you, I have noticed."

"Then what happened?" demanded Sara, eagerly.

"Lord Carville sent me off to fetch his breakfast and he said when I was done with that, I was to come roust you from bed and tell you that he wanted to see you straight away. And that's what I done."

With Daisy's help, Sara dressed quickly and was out the door and down the corridor to Philip's room with surprising speed. Knowing she was expected, she gave a peremptory knock on the door and entered. She was halfway across the room to the bed before she realized that Hugh was in the room, too.

A spark of warmth leapt to life within her at the sight of him. He was, if possible, looking even more handsome, even more commanding than ever and she cast him a smile that, she was sure, contained a full portion of affection and admiration.

The look he in return directed at her was less promising. He bowed slightly and wished her a good morning, but there was in his manner none of the ease or affection it had been her privilege to witness the night before. His demeanor was cordial yet cool and she was immediately set on her guard.

Her gaze flew from Hugh to Philip, then back again. "Have I interrupted your conversation? Shall I come back another time?"

"Not at all," said Hugh. "I was leaving just now, as a matter of fact. Carville, I shall visit you later to ensure that all has gone well." With another slight bow and a mere passing glance toward Sara, he was gone.

His tone was so abrupt and his departure so unexpected, that Sara blurted, "Something has gone horridly wrong, hasn't it! Oh, Philip, what could have occurred to cause Mr. Deverill to behave so?"

Philip hiked himself up in the bed against some pillows and summoned Sara to move closer. "Nothing has occurred, so don't go firing yourself out of a cannon, you silly girl! Here, come and sit beside me on the bed. I've been waiting for you all morning."

Sara did as she was told and, sitting down upon the bed, her blue eyes scanned her brother's countenance. He was looking quite rested; his color had improved, as had his disposition. "You're looking much better," she remarked. "You must have passed a good night."

"I did, indeed. After you left me last night I started in

to thinking and it helped clear my head of a good many things, I can tell you! Why, I haven't slept as well in a month as I did last night.''

"Then I am glad to hear of it. Tell me, what were you thinking about?''

"You. And I've come to a decision, Sara. You might not chime in with it, but I hope you'll be a good girl and obey me nevertheless.''

"Now I am alarmed!'' she said, laughing. "Very well! Let me hear of this decision!''

"The thing of it is, Sara, I'm—I'm sending you away. I'm sending you to Bath to stay with Westbury and his mother.''

"Oh, no, you are not!'' she exclaimed, deeply agitated. She sprang to her feet. "I am *not* leaving Carvington Hall!''

"Oh, yes! Yes, you are most certainly! I've already set Daisy to packing your trunks!''

"Then you may just set Daisy to *un*packing them, Philip, for I refuse! Do you hear me? There is no good reason that I should leave my home!''

"Yes, there is! Your staying here in a household of men puts your reputation very much on the line, my girl!''

"What are you talking about?'' she demanded, crossing her arms and fixing him with a hard stare.

"I am speaking of your good name, Miss Sassy, so I'll thank you not to adopt that tone with me, if you please! Only think on what I'm saying to you: aside from a maid or two, you're living in a household full of men. No one but Deverill and Hetherington think you to be the house-keeper, which means the entire neighborhood has observed that there are bachelors in the house, but no chaperone for you!''

Sara gave her head a slight shake. "But Philip—''

"Just listen to me, please! In a day or two or three, perhaps, Deverill and Hetherington will be gone and you'll have no more reason to pose as a servant. But the town won't know that, you see. They'll know only that you lived in a house for weeks on end with three bachelors. What then do you think your prospects will be?''

"My—my prospects?" she repeated with a slight laugh of astonishment. "Philip, I am barely nineteen years, just home from school and already you have me married off!"

"Laugh, if you like, but we'll see how hard you laugh when no one invites you to any of those precious assemblies you've set your heart on attending! There! That caught your attention, didn't it?''

Sara sat slowly back down on the bed. "I can hardly credit—Philip, are you certain?"

"Of course I am. Dash it, Sara! Don't you know there is an entire gaggle of geese just like you in town, and every last one of them has a mother with an eye to marrying her daughter off well. Those women wouldn't think twice about narrowing the competition and eliminating all comers by tattling tales. Once word of your situation becomes known, you'd be out of the running in a heartbeat, Sara, and no mistake!''

"But certainly no one would bear tales about me! After all, I may have stayed in a house of bachelors, but our relationships have remained quite innocent." No sooner did those words leave her mouth, than Sara looked quickly away, lest her brother should see the fiery blushes that suddenly mantled her cheeks.

She recognized her words to be little more than lies, for her behavior with Hugh Deverill had been far from innocent, as well she knew. But she couldn't very well admit such a thing to her brother. She said, instead, "Philip, please don't feel you are obliged to do this.''

"Well, of course I am obliged! You're my sister, after all, and it's up to me to look after you, when all is said and done. Of course, the whole notion never occurred to me. I didn't see the hubbub at all until Deverill put me in the way of it. If anyone is an expert on reputations, it's Devil Deverill!''

Again did Sara leap from the bed. "Are you telling me that Mr. Deverill came up with this scheme? Mr. Deverill told you I must leave the house?"

"Not in so many words, no. But he did bring to my mind that a girl has nothing but her reputation to stake her future on—that, and an inheritance, of course! But thanks to me, you've no inheritance at all left you and so your reputation must be protected at all costs! At least, that's the way I see the business."

"But, Philip—"

"Dammit, Sara, I won't be dissuaded! It's time you started looking to me as the head of this family and do as I say. Westbury's carriage will call for you at two o'clock, so I suggest you make yourself ready by then, Miss Sassy.''

Thereafter, no amount of argument Sara put forth could change her brother's mind. No tears or recriminations could convince him that she should be allowed to stay. In the end, it was his mention of Hugh Deverill that finally caused Sara to accede to her brother's demand.

No sooner had Philip mentioned Hugh's name, than Sara was forcibly reminded of what had passed between them the night before. Since the moment she had left the library and he had closed the door upon her, Hugh Deverill had been to her a different man. His manner toward Sara this very morning had not so much as hinted at any of the tenderness or feelings he had shown her last evening. In fact, now that she thought on it, she realized he had not been at all happy to see her, nor had he displayed any trace of the affection she hoped he felt for her; the same affection she felt in her heart for him.

And now, it appeared he had contrived to convince Philip that she was to be sent away. Were she gone from

Carvington Hall, he would not have to look at her; he
would not be reminded of her fast and very unladylike
behavior in the library.

To Sara's way of thinking, that could only mean that he
was quite disgusted with her conduct and had convinced
Philip that only a young woman of suspect reputation could
behave as wantonly as she. A faint memory of Daisy's warning of cows and milk and pennies came to Sara's mind in
a confused rush. How she had laughed at Daisy but now
she wished she had listened to her warning; now she wished
she had never allowed Hugh Deverill to take her in his
arms.

It was a hard thing to understand that a man could hold
her and kiss her as tenderly as Hugh had in an evening
of love, only to wish to be rid of her come the light of day.
Having long since realized that she had tumbled quite
hopelessly in love with Hugh, she could only suppose he
could behave so because he did not return her regard.

This notion sent her tearfully rushing from Philip's bed-
side to her own room and only when she had the door
safely closed to protect her privacy did she give herself up
to all her turbulent emotions.

But her privacy was shattered by the presence of Daisy,
who was engaged in carrying out Philip's instructions. No
sooner did the first sob of strong emotion escape Sara's
lips, than Daisy abandoned her packing to wrap an arm
about her mistress's shoulders and lead her to a chair near
the window. "There, there, miss! You mustn't cry so!"

"Oh, Daisy! I am to leave Carvington Hall and all because
of that beastly man!" cried Sara.

"Now, which beastly man do you mean, miss? Certainly,
not Lord Carville, I should think! And since Lord Westbury
hasn't a beastly bone in his body, I must suppose you
mean only Mr. Deverill. Is that who you were talking about,
miss?"

Sara sniffed audibly and nodded her head.

"Now, miss, you don't truly in your heart believe him to be beastly, now do you? No, and not when anyone can see he thinks the world and all of you or he wouldn't be quite so concerned about your good name, now, would he?" asked Daisy, reasonably.

"Oh, Daisy, you don't understand!" sobbed Sara.

"I understand a good deal more than you may think, miss. But most of all, I understand that you are to leave the house at two o'clock and if you don't stop your crying straight away, you'll be saying goodbye to your brother with puffy eyes and a red nose."

These words of sense had a powerful effect. Sara sprang to her feet and rushed to view her reflection in the mirror on her dressing table. In an instant did she see that Daisy was right; her face bore all the signs of tears and torment.

As if divining her thoughts, Daisy pressed a freshly-pressed handkerchief into her hand. "I'll just fetch some fresh cool water for you to rinse those eyes with, miss. You'll be wanting a cucumber, too, I think, to take some of that redness away. Leave it all to me."

Weary from fighting with her brother, and rather heart-worn by the realization of Hugh's treachery, Sara placed herself in Daisy's capable hands. The devices Daisy assembled to repair the damage left by tears were effective, and it was a pale yet presentable Sara who knocked on Philip's bedroom door just before two o'clock that afternoon.

She was dressed for traveling in a pelisse and bonnet of rose that very fetchingly framed her face and lent an uncommonly lovely hue to her pale complexion. She stepped into the room and the color drained further from her face: Hugh was standing near the window, his back to the panes of glass, and his face in shadow.

His expression she could not discern; his pose was indecipherable. She did know, however, that he made no move toward her nor did he speak any words of affection, comfort or farewell. Her surprise at seeing him dwindled into flushing embarrassment.

"Come here, then!" commanded Philip from the bed. He was propped up against an assortment of pillows and his expression was stern as if he expected further protest from her. "Are you all packed, then? Good. Westbury should be along any moment. Like all men of dull conversation and excellent character, he is punctual in the extreme!"

"If you dislike him so, why must I go to him?" asked Sara in a woebegone voice.

"Sara, we have been through all this. You need a gooseberry to lend you countenance; someone to take you in hand and make a lady of you at long last as that school of yours tried to do. Old Lady Westbury will fit the bill. She'll set the gossips back on their heels and she'll see that your good name is restored you."

Sara had long since passed the point where she was capable of further argument. Once again did her emotions come the fore, and her lip trembled threateningly. She managed to say, "Yes, Philip," but those words were uttered in such a tremulous, emotional fashion that her brother stirred uncomfortably.

"Here, now, Sara! Let's have none of that," he said, in some alarm. "Why, you should be glad of this. Only think of all the assemblies and routs you've been pestering me to take you to. Lady Westbury shall see that you attend them, and that you enjoy yourself for a change."

Gladly would Sara have foregone balls and assemblies if only she could remain with Philip and Hugh at Carvington Hall, and so she considered saying. But she didn't think Philip would be at all receptive to such a scheme. In his expression she saw a trace of annoyance that told her he was fast growing impatient with her tears and entreaties. Hugh's expression, she saw, was not any more sympathetic.

He had stepped away from the window and rounded the bed. As he approached her, she saw that his countenance was guarded as if he were holding himself in check.

In his eyes Sara saw no indication of tenderness or affection. When she chanced to recall that it was Hugh's idea that she be sent away from Carvington Hall, she realized just how grave an error in judgment she had made. It was swiftly borne upon her that by returning Hugh's kisses in the library, she had committed a solecism from which she might never be forgiven; that by returning his embrace and thereby revealing the depth of her feelings for Hugh, she had instead repelled him. His expression and demeanor proclaimed the truth she had hitherto failed to recognize: Hugh Deverill did not love her. It was a wound to her heart from which she thought she would never recover.

Hugh continued to approach her, his gaze unwavering and his blue eyes as still and cold as a winter morning. By contrast, Sara's own eyes filled suddenly with tears, and she looked quickly away, fearful that he might have noticed them.

"Make your goodbyes, then, like a good girl," commanded Philip.

Gladly would she have done so, for a proper goodbye would have meant throwing her arms about her brother and kissing his cheek and sobbingly telling him how much she would miss him while she was gone. But with Hugh Deverill in the room, watching her every move with frowning fixity, she could not very well do such a thing. He still believed her to be the housekeeper; a housekeeper who, only the night before, had thrown herself at him in the library and clung to him like a piece of amorous ivy.

The unfairness of her circumstance caused the tears to

gather in Sara's eyes again. However, she managed to bite back the sudden swell of emotion and dip a very creditable curtsy. When next she raised her eyes, she beheld the figure of Hugh Deverill standing very close upon her.

Without thinking, she held out her hand to him; he took it, and held it fast for a moment. That gave her the courage to say, "Goodbye, Mr. Deverill. You—you will take good care of my—of Lord Carville, won't you? You will see that his foot heals properly?"

"It shall be done, Sara."

"And—and will you call at Lord Westbury's home in Bath? Will you visit me with news of how Philip goes on?" She hated herself for being reduced to such a state; she hated herself for begging for just one more chance to see him, but so great was her desire to detect some sign of gentleness in his expression, she could not help herself. She saw him hesitate in his reply and her slim, gloved fingers tightened impulsively about his. "Please?"

"Of course," he murmured at last.

"I shall take that as a promise. You—you won't forget, will you? You have never before failed in any promise you have made me."

She thought he looked a bit surprised, then she saw the ghost of a smile on his lips. "I shall not fail you, Sara." With her hand still in his, Hugh guided her to the door and out into the hallway.

Like a drowning man, Sara gratefully grasped at the implication of such a gesture. Surely, she reasoned, he meant to speak at long last of the reason behind his uncommon and hurtful behavior. Surely they needed only a moment alone together, away from probing eyes and curious ears, and he would explain himself.

But Hugh took advantage of no such opportunity. Without a word, he led Sara down the stairs to the front hall, and no sooner did they reach that destination than a footman opened the front door to admit Lord Westbury. He swept his hat from his head as he came in, smiling and in an excellent humor.

Ignoring Hugh altogether, he said, pleasantly, "Sara! That's a fetching bonnet! You look quite lovely this afternoon." He held out his hand and directed a challenging look at Hugh.

Without hesitation or protest did Hugh Deverill relinquish his hold on Sara. He placed her hand in Lord Westbury's with no more emotion than he would have handed over one of those wretched gaming vowels he was so keen on collecting.

Feeling sick with misery, Sara was unsure she could trust herself to speak without bursting into tears, but she nevertheless managed to say, "You won't forget your promise to me! Say you will not!"

"Promise?" echoed Lord Westbury, brightly. "What promise is that?"

"Mr. Deverill has promised to visit me and bring me news of Carvington Hall. You won't forget, will you?"

"Of course not," Hugh said, in a tone that afforded not the least emotion. He was, she saw, holding himself once again in rigid check, as he had earlier in Philip's bed chamber. His mouth was set in a firm line and his eyes, as they looked down upon her, were hooded, making it impossible for her to discern any hint of what his feelings may be.

Lord Westbury smiled again. "Yes, Deverill, come visit, come as often as you like. You shall probably not find us at home, but you will be welcome to call, nevertheless. Come along, Sara. My mother is anxious to see you again."

With these mild words, Lord Westbury led Sara away toward his waiting carriage.

Chapter Sixteen

Sara waited for the sound of the knocker on the door of Westbury house for three days. While the knocker did sound for various visitors, all of whom proved to be among the cream of Bath society, none of those visitors turned out to be the one person she most particularly wanted to see.

Steadfastly did she believe that Hugh Deverill would visit her. So sure was Sara that Hugh's arrival at Westbury House was imminent, she politely declined every invitation put before her to venture out of the house. Instead she took to passing time in a chair drawn near the drawing room window that looked out over the street.

Still he did not come. Despite her hopefulness, despite the promise he had made her, Hugh Deverill made no appearance at Westbury House. As each day passed with still no sign of him, Sara's spirits plummeted a little bit more, but still she would not abandon her place by the front window.

Both Lord Westbury and his mother took care to leave Sara to nurse her wounds in her own way, but on the afternoon of the third day, Lady Westbury entered the drawing room and remarked, "A girl could waste away to dust sitting in that chair day after day. You had best come with me to the Pump Room, miss, for you're in need of some color in your cheeks. Don't think I shall allow you to fob me off with one of your weak excuses. Today I shall not allow no for an answer!"

Lady Westbury proved to be true to her word and within the hour, Sara was indeed whisked away to the Pump Room. Lord Westbury accompanied them, and upon their arrival, he handed first his mother then Sara down from the carriage with gratifying care.

They entered the Pump Room to find it crowded with visitors of all ages and sizes. At one end of the large, spacious hall a small band of musicians played a soothing melody that could scarce be heard over the hubbub of conversation from the assembled guests.

Lady Westbury, a veteran of daily visits to the place over the course of many years, led the way to a sunny alcove on one side of the room and dispatched her son in the direction of the serving tables.

"You shall drink a glass of the waters with me, Sara," commanded her ladyship. "Mind you, it must be drunk hot, for it is that way in which you shall receive the most good."

"But I enjoy an excellent health, ma'am," said Sara, mildly.

"Do you? Then perhaps you would be good enough to explain the paleness of your skin or the decided lack of a sparkle in your eye! You don't look the least bit healthy to me! Why, when I was a girl, I was seven times more lively, you may be assured!"

Lord Westbury returned bearing three glasses full of

water, the color of which was far from clear. Sara looked doubtfully at it. "I must confess I have never before drunk a glass of Bath water before."

"Then perhaps it is time you should start," recommended her ladyship after partaking of a hearty quaff. "I drink two pints of the stuff a day and you won't find me sulking alone in a chair by the window."

Sara felt herself blushing to the roots of her hair. "I— I didn't think you would have noticed anything I did!"

"I may be old, but I'm not precisely stupid," said Lady Westbury, with unnerving candor. She drank deeply once more from her glass before saying, "Far be it from me to pry into the business of a girl who wishes to waste her life away in my drawing room when she could be larking about the town with people of her own ken and age! Do as you like! But don't think *I* shall bear you company! *I* have balls and assemblies to attend! *I* have friends and acquaintances who demand my attention."

One such acquaintance, an elderly woman who was seated at a table some distance away along with several other people, caught Lady Westbury's eye with a beckoning wave. "There!" said her ladyship as she thrust her empty glass at her son. "I'm off to speak with Lady Sutcliffe. Mind you drink that glass up, miss! I won't think kindly of bringing you back to Westbury house in the same fit of dismals in which you left it!"

Lord Westbury waited until his mother was safely out of earshot before saying, "Don't think you must drink the stuff, if you don't wish to, Sara. My mother means well, but you musn't let her bully you into doing something you'd as lief not."

She cast him a rather rueful look. "I suppose I hadn't realized how beastly I've behaved since I came to you. Have I been ungrateful? Is your mother very much disappointed in me?"

"Not at all," he said, with a kind smile. "She may not wish to show it, but I think she likes you very much."

"I am glad to hear it! I would not wish her to think me rude or so ungrateful for her kindness that she would wish to send me packing!"

Lord Westbury placed his hand over hers and said, in a quiet voice of deep sincerity, "I should never let her!"

She was surprised and for a moment she could do little more than stand there, feeling the pressure of his fingers on hers. Her blue eyes met his with a questioning expression and his hand fell slowly away.

He said, after a moment in which they stood in awkward silence, "You know, nothing would please my mother more than to have someone like you to take about. It would make her attendance at the assemblies much more entertaining. Only think how much she enjoyed the evening we all spent together at the theater!"

"As did I! Both you and your mother were very kind," said Sara, politely.

"Would you object if we were to show you such kindness again?" asked his lordship, gently. "There is an assembly tomorrow evening at the Upper Rooms that I think you should enjoy very much. And I see, even now, a number of young acquaintances of mine here in the Pump Room who should prove quite diverting were I to introduce you to them. What do you say, Sara? Can I persuade you to abandon your vigil by the front window in favor of accompanying my mother?"

It was clear to Sara that both Lord Westbury and his mother had her best interests at heart. Over the course of the last three days, in which she had been forced to come to the slow and sad conclusion that Hugh Deverill was probably not at all likely to visit her, despite his promise, she had fallen into a state of some depression.

Indeed, up until the moment she had passed through

the doors of the Pump Room, she had been aware of a growing threat that she might, at any given time, suddenly burst into a storm of tears born of bitter disappointment and unforgivable betrayal. She had, indeed, moped about Westbury House, refusing to go out or participate in any entertainment put before her. Within the confines of the walls of Westbury House, she could think only of Hugh Deverill and the pain of the unrequited love she felt for him. So acute was her despondency, that she realized for the first time that her society must have been dull in the extreme, her conversation, monosyllabic, to the point that she rather thought Lady Westbury had grown quite disgusted with her.

But then Sara had entered the Pump Room and a most curious thing had occurred: no sooner had she passed through the tall, double doors of that establishment, than she began to feel a trifle better, if only for the simple reason that her thoughts had been diverted from dwelling upon Hugh. Oh, she still found that her gaze strayed about the room from time to time, seeking a glimpse of him among the throngs of people in attendance. Yet she did know some relief from the melancholy that had plagued her for the past three days.

There was, she knew, some bit of truth in Lord Westbury's suggestion that she abandon her solitary vigil by the drawing room window for the more diverting prospect of going about in society. She could not continue on for very much longer in the same dispirited state in which she had dwelt for the past few days. She knew, too, that since she had removed to Westbury House, both Lord Westbury and his mother had done their best to please her and she had been so caught up in her own misery, she had failed to show the least gratitude.

"Well, Sara?" prompted his lordship. "Shall I introduce

you to that group of young people I see gathered by the serving tables?''

Now determined to meet his kindness with the greatest civility, Sara forced a smile and summoned her spirit to respond to Lord Westbury's words. "Yes, you may, but only if you will say I shall not be compelled to drink any of this horrid water!"

He laughed and took the glass from her. "That's a good girl. I knew you could do it. Come along, then. I shall make you known to some young friends of mine."

Those friends to whom he introduced her proved a lively and happy group and in their company Sara's thoughts were again diverted from dwelling upon Hugh Deverill.

Those same young friends appeared at the assembly in the Upper Rooms the very next evening. No sooner did Sara cross the threshold in the wake of Lord Westbury and his mother, than her attention was claimed by the friends she had made in the Pump Room and she was carried off to a corner of the room occupied by even more people of her own age.

Some short time later, Sara found herself thoroughly entrenched in the center of the little group. When the orchestra sounded and a country set was formed, she found herself in the gratifying position of having to choose one dance partner from several who applied for her hand.

She danced every dance, and if she could not say that her melancholy had completely disappeared, she could certainly admit that it had abated sufficiently to have earned her a modicum of praise from the other guests as a pretty-behaved young girl.

Throughout the evening she was aware of Lord Westbury's constant regard. Indeed, on more than one occasion she happened to look up to find his gaze upon her and a slight smile of appreciation touching his lips. On each occasion did she smile back, for she found his solid presence comforting in an evening full of new experiences.

She danced an energetic country jig with a young man who had proved himself to be most attentive. He escorted her back to her circle of new friends, where she had to make a conscious effort to resist a temptation to ply her fan with vigor. A more acceptable and lady-like method for cooling her heated brow came in the form of a glass of punch, presented to her by yet another admiring young man. Sara drank it gratefully and was handing the glass back to the gentleman when a chance look in the direction of the door caused her heart to leap up into her throat.

There in the doorway stood Hugh Deverill, with Lord Hetherington at his side. If possible, he was looking more handsome, more commanding, than she had ever before seen him. He was staring at her, his brow furrowed in concentration and his blue eyes fixed upon her with unnerving intensity. She almost jumped out of her shoes, so unexpected was his presence and so alien her reaction to it. With her heart pounding in her breast, she waited, quite unable to move, to see what he might do next. She dreaded the thought that he might make his way toward her as much as she prayed that he would do so. When he turned and spoke briefly to Lord Hetherington, and took a step in her direction, she quite thought she might never take a decent breath again in her life.

Indeed, it appeared very much as if Hugh Deverill had every intention of charting a direct course across the dance floor to Sara's side. He might have well done so, were it not for Lord Westbury's interference.

He had been watching Sara all evening with ever-deepening appreciation. No smile that graced her lips had escaped his notice, no frown on her smooth brow had appeared that he had not instantly wished to erase it. He had, therefore, not failed to notice the expression of utter shock that had drained her face of color the moment she had perceived Hugh Deverill's presence.

Westbury immediately made his way to Hugh's side and said, in a lowered tone that was, nevertheless effectively belligerent, "Deverill! How the devil did you get in here?"

Hugh met his angry gaze with cool composure. "I paid for a ticket, just like everyone else, of course."

"Ticket or no, I'm astonished you were allowed to gain entrance! What are you doing here, as if I could not figure it out for myself!"

Hugh flicked him a glance of dislike. "I should rather think you might. I've always considered you dull-witted in the extreme, but I never thought you precisely stupid."

"Have a care," his lordship warned. "My mother and I have gone a long way to scotch any rumors about your dealings with Sara. Don't ruin it now!"

But Hugh hardly paid him the least heed. He had done his best to stay away, knowing very well that it was in Sara's best interest that he do so. In the three days that had passed since she left Carvington Hall, he had done little else but think of her and the decisions he had been forced to make on her behalf. It had fallen to Hugh to take her scape-grace brother in hand, and make him see the sense of protecting her reputation. And it had fallen to Hugh to endure the ultimate sacrifice of handing her over to the one man who might possibly stand in some chance of securing her affections. So, too, had it fallen to Hugh ensure that there never be another occasion where he could so lose control of himself as he had done that night in the library.

It had been a mistake to have allowed her to stay with him that evening, for he hadn't realized until that night

just how much he cared for her. Indeed, what had begun
as a mere flirtation with Sara, a diversion calculated to pass
the time at a dull-as-tombs country house, had somehow,
without his being aware, grown into something much more
meaningful.

During the course of the last three days he had come
to know his own mind where she was concerned, and he
recognized that his feelings had progressed far beyond the
point of mere attraction. He was in love with Sara and
realized that he must have been so even while he had
plotted to send her away to protect her reputation. Common sense told him that he had been successful in protecting her; he knew, too, he could continue to shield her
only by staying far enough away so his name might never
be linked with hers.

But common sense proved no match for the lure of
Hugh's feelings for Sara. He convinced himself that he
had to see her—just once!—that he might then be satisfied
and stay away forever. But no sooner had he crossed the
threshold of the front room at the Upper Assembly and
spied her smiling and happy and animated, than his resolu-
tion fell by the wayside.

He was dimly aware of the orchestra striking the first
chords of the next dance. Without thinking he took a step
toward Sara, only to feel Lord Westbury's steadying hand
on his sleeve, halting his progress before it was begun.

"Deverill, have you gone daft?" demanded his lordship.
"The orchestra is about to play a waltz!"

"I shouldn't care if they were about to play their scales!"
Hugh retorted, in deep annoyance.

Lord Westbury clutched at his sleeve again. "You cannot
waltz with Sara. You cannot be seen to be on such intimate
terms. Only think of what you'll do to her."

But Hugh was thinking precisely that. He shook off Westbury's hold upon his sleeve and made his way to Sara's side.

Sara watched his approach with an ever-quickening heartbeat and when he stood in front of her and bowed and held out his hand, so great were the emotions raging within her that she thought her seriously weakened legs might fail to support her. She had, as it happened, nothing to worry over in that regard, for she followed Hugh onto the dance floor with credible grace.

Just as he had that evening in the long gallery at Carvington Hall, Hugh slipped his arm about Sara's slim waist and began to waltz her about the room.

The feeling of his arms around her, the thrill of moving with rapid, exhilarating grace over the floor, was a potent experience. All Sara's despondency, all final traces of hurt she had suffered over the last three days, fell by the wayside and Sara gave herself up to the wonder of finding herself in Hugh's arms once more.

He held her close, whisking her into every turn, reveling in the feel of her. She danced with him as if they had danced together always and he was a little astonished to realize how right, how natural she felt in his arms—and by the realization that he wanted her to remain so forever.

The music ended much too soon for Hugh's purposes. Gladly would he have danced with Sara for hours on end, but as the final note sounded, he tucked her hand in the crook of his elbow and escorted her to Lady Westbury's side.

He encountered in that elderly lady's expression a look of fury; in Lord Westbury's eye he caught a minatory gleam.

With perfect composure, Hugh bowed slightly and brought Sara's hand to his lips.

Hugh left the assembly immediately thereafter and no sooner did he step outside onto the street and take a deep breath of clear night air than he realized his mistake. He had never before been one to allow his heart to rule his head but he had done so in this case.

It had been wrong to have danced with her, but it had been disastrous to have waltzed with her. He had seen the looks on some of the faces of the people in attendance; judgmental looks, critical looks, that told him that Sara would no doubt suffer the consequences of his actions.

For her part, Sara worried that her behavior might cause Hugh some suffering. He had left her at Lady Westbury's side, who in great agitation, ordered her carriage to be brought straight away. Not until they were settled within that vehicle and they were driving the short distance back to Westbury House did Sara dare to speak.

She looked from Lord Westbury to his mother and asked, "Why are you so angry with me? Pray, what have I done?"

Quite unable to speak, Lady Westbury had to be content to simply cast her young charge a look of fury.

Lord Westbury, in better command of his emotions, said, in a voice of strong censure, "You have, I'm afraid, committed a grave error, Sara. You should never have danced with Deverill, that much is clear, but to have danced a waltz—"

"Oh, there's no good in berating the girl," interrupted his mother. "She didn't know. How could she when she hasn't got a mother to guide her?"

"But why should I not have danced with Mr. Deverill?" asked Sara. "Why was it so wrong?"

Lord Westbury leaned toward her a bit and said, in a gentler tone than he had used before, "It wasn't so much that you danced with Hugh Deverill—although I might have wished that you would have engaged a more suitable partner! No, the mischief was that you danced with Hugh Deverill and together you danced a waltz."

"Was that wrong of me?" asked Sara in a small voice.

"Lord, yes!" retorted her ladyship. "Yes, it was, but you couldn't know that, I'm sure."

Judging from the troubled look that marred Lord Westbury's expression, Sara divined that her disgrace at having committed such a faux-pas was significant. She said, earnestly, "I promise I shall not do it again."

"But don't you see, child? The damage is already done. I fear you will not be attending any more assemblies for a while."

Sara looked at Lord Westbury with eyes gone wide. At the time Hugh had taken her in his arms, she hadn't known that she was committing a social solecism. But had she known, she doubted very much that she might have behaved differently. Her dance with Hugh had been one of the most enjoyable experiences of her life. Gladly would she give up a lifetime of assemblies for one single dance with Hugh. Happily would she throw to the winds a lifetime of social acceptance for the feel of Hugh's strong and comforting arms about her.

But she dared not mention such musings to either Lord Westbury or his mother. They still both had about them rather grim expressions that told Sara just how wretched they thought her situation to be and she hadn't the heart to tell them otherwise.

The carriage drew up at last before Westbury House. In the hall, Lady Westbury declined to lay off her cape and gloves, and abruptly took to the stairs. "I'm going to bed, although I doubt very much I shall earn a wink of sleep!" she said, querulously.

Lord Westbury watched her ascent up the stairs. "Good night, Mother. I shall see you in the morning."

"I doubt it!" she snapped over her shoulder.

He assisted Sara out of her cloak. "She didn't mean that, you know. She shall be in better spirits tomorrow, after a good night's rest. We all shall!"

"Do you think she will ever forgive me? Do you think she believes that I truly didn't know I was doing wrong?"

"I think she'll forgive you. As to your other question, I don't know. Tell me, Sara, didn't you have an inkling of a notion that dancing at a public assembly with Hugh Deverill—a man of his reputation!—could not possibly be in your best interests?"

Sara dipped her head a moment, on the pretext of removing her gloves. "No one has ever told me so," she said evasively, "and tonight was, after all, my first time attending a public assembly. Truly, I never meant to deceive anyone!"

"No, I don't think you meant to deceive. But I think you meant to dance with Deverill, no matter what the consequences." That remark brought Sara's head up with snap. "Ah, I see I am correct. No, don't look away, my dear, for you have nothing to fear from me. I won't scold you and I see no point in trying to persuade you to change your mind. You are not, after all, the first young woman to fall in love with Hugh Deverill. I fear the mischief is, though, that you shall not be the last."

"No, you cannot be right, I know. Why, Mr. Deverill is not at all the sort of man you think he is."

He could have debated with her; he could have given her any number of arguments to convince her that Hugh Deverill was not the man of her imaginings. He refrained

from doing so, for in Sara's eyes he saw all the telltale signs
of a young woman in love.

She was, of course, in love with a man who was most
undeserving of her regard, but she was in love, nonetheless.
Even more curious to Lord Westbury was his suspicion that
Hugh Deverill returned Sara's regard. He had seen it in
Hugh's eyes when first Hugh had spied Sara at the assem-
bly; he had recognized it in Hugh's purposeful disregard
for the proprieties in favor of a few stolen moments in
Sara's company.

Lord Westbury didn't know if Hugh had yet come to
recognize the depths of his feelings for Sara, but to his
lordship's way of thinking, it was only a matter of time
before he did so. Then it would remain to be seen if Devil
Deverill, one of society's great *roués*, would act upon those
feelings.

It was a little bit comforting to know that Sara Brandon-
Howe had managed to whiten the heart of England's fore-
most blackguard yet, at the same time, Lord Westbury knew
that nothing good would ever come of the affection Sara
and Hugh held for each other. Somehow, in some way,
he was certain that Hugh Deverill would manage to hurt
Sara. When that happened, he intended to be on hand to
comfort her and steer her into his own waiting arms.

Chapter Seventeen

Sara spent the morning following the disastrous assembly in her customary chair by the window, her feet tucked up under her. Her attention was half focused on the book of poetry she held in her lap, and half on the passing traffic on the street outside.

She was now convinced more than ever that she was deeply in love with Hugh Deverill. She now thought it was also beyond question that he, in turn, cared for her. Certainly, he was attracted to her, for when their eyes met and he smiled at her ever so slightly in that way he had, she saw in his expression a warmth and a pleasure that she did not detect whenever he chanced to look upon another.

But she also knew that, despite the attraction she recognized in his eyes, he could be quite hard-hearted, else he would not have stayed away as long as he had. She could not make up her mind if it had been luck or design that had brought them together last night at the assembly; she hoped with all her heart that he had sought her out and that he would do so again by coming to Westbury House that morning.

But when the Westbury's butler opened the door to announce the arrival of a visitor, it was not Hugh who entered the room, but Philip. He hobbled toward her, supported on two canes, looking rather pleased to see her.

Sara was equally glad and immediately rushed to him. She threw her arms about his neck, hugging him wholeheartedly. "Thank heavens you have come at last!"

"Well, if you aren't the greatest piece of nonsense!" he said, laughing and staggering a bit under the weight of her onslaught. "Always mussing my waistcoats, that's what you are, Miss Sassy!"

"Oh, Philip, I am so happy to see you! Please, may I come home now? Please?"

He gave her cheek a light cuff. "Not yet, but soon, I should think. No, now don't pout! It don't become you by half!"

"Yes, Philip, but I should dearly love to return to my own home."

"Westbury isn't treating you ill, is he?" asked Philip feeling a sudden and unaccustomed swell of guardianship. "Or Lady Westbury? She hasn't been cruel to you, has she?"

"No, Philip. Both Lord Westbury and his mother have been very kind to me. It is only . . ." Sara considered confiding to him the events of the night before and just as swiftly did she discard that notion, saying, instead, "It is only that I miss you terribly."

There was something about her tone, gone rather sad and unsure, that caught his attention. He watched her a moment with uncommon scrutiny and he thought he detected a hint of troubled uncertainty in her expression. He did not, however, press that point. Being a rather self-centered young man, he wasn't entirely certain he wanted to know the cause behind his sister's distress. For if he knew the cause, he might have to act on it, and that would seriously upset his plans for the day.

He said, in a voice falsely bright, "Here, now, Sara! Let me tell you why I've come, for I haven't much time. Deverill drove me, you know."

"Mr. Deverill? He drove you here to Westbury House and—and he didn't come in?"

"No, and it's just as well, for I don't wish him to hang on any of my words. Listen, Sara, I must needs ask you about those dratted vowels of mine. You know, the ones I told you about. I wrote them all down in a little ledger book that I carried with me right here." He patted his hand over the breast pocket of his coat and said, "I'll be dashed if I can find the book anywhere! It's gone! Vanished! I was half-hoping you might have taken it."

"Me? But, why would I have done so?"

"Well, you did spout a whale's tale about handling everything with Deverill. For all I know, you might have taken the blasted book so you would know just how much blunt I owed everyone. I thought you might have wanted it so you could negotiate with Deverill a plan for paying off some of my debts."

She shook her head slightly. "Philip, I never knew you had such a book, and I assure you, I never knew where you kept it."

"Oh!" said Philip, rather stunned. He sank down onto a nearby chair and thought a moment, then said, with a smile that was more brave than sincere, "I was rather afraid you'd say that! Well, you might as well know, we're done for now! If Deverill holds my gaming vouchers and he has my ledger book that lists everyone else to whom I owe money, I dare say it's the end for us!"

"Why, Philip?" asked Sara, though unsure she wanted

to know the answer. "Why is our circumstance so dire if, indeed, Mr. Deverill has possession of your ledger book?"

"Because then he'll know exactly how much money I owe and to whom, that's why! I told you once before, I think the fellow has been buying up my vowels. I know for certain he settled my debts in Bath, and I'm equally certain he didn't do so out of the goodness of his heart!"

"But what other reason could he have, then, Philip? Why should Mr. Deverill wish to know the particulars of your debts?"

Again did Philip pause before answering, as if he were weighing the prudence of confiding the entire truth to his sister. At last, he said, rather forlornly, "I dare say he wants to take possession of Carvington Hall. He did tell me once that he was in mind of finding just such an estate for himself. I—I can't prove it, Sara, but I rather suspect he holds the paper on the mortgage I took out on the old place. If he has also bought up all my other debts, he'll be in the perfect position to offer me some shamefully low price for the Hall—and I shall be in the position of being forced to accept it!"

"He would never do such a thing!" Sara protested, in a weak voice. "Surely Mr. Deverill would never be so mean-spirited as to drive us from our home!"

"I should never presume to guess what Deverill will or will not do," said Philip, "although I've no doubt he can be ruthless! Any man who can fleece innocents at the gaming tables as he does must be so!"

Now most thoroughly alarmed, Sara took a halting, agitated turn about the room. Her heart refused to believe anything her brother had said. She was too much in love with Hugh Deverill to think such ill of him, yet a nagging voice in the back of her mind she had hitherto managed to ignore came to the fore, insisting that she recognize the truth in Philip's words.

Hugh was, she knew, capable of such behavior. He had certainly been cold-hearted when he had escorted her from the library after kissing her senseless. And she had good reason to suspect Hugh Deverill to be the person who had orchestrated her banishment from Carvington Hall just so Philip would be unprotected and completely under his control. Now it seemed that he had contrived to mastermind their financial ruin merely so he might take possession of their ancestral home.

Just as surely as she was convinced a scant five minutes earlier of Mr. Deverill's affection, Sara now realized that he had probably never felt the least fondness for her. If indeed his goal all along had been to possess Carvington Hall, he could not have picked a more willing accomplice than she to help in his quest. Oh, she saw it all so clearly, now! He had made up to her, beguiled her, flattered her. With little more sense than a stupid, romantic schoolgirl, she had succumbed to his charms. She felt mightily used, indeed.

Sara sank down onto a chair near her brother and said, in a voice of mingled emotion, "Oh, Philip! He *is* capable of such behavior! Mr. Deverill *is* just as cold-hearted as you described!"

"Whatever his demands may be, I fear we shall have to give in to them," said Philip, pessimistically. "Lord knows *I* haven't any way of raising any brass!"

"But we cannot give in to him! We mustn't allow him to take our home from us, Philip. Perhaps we could sell something—some paintings from the gallery or silver plate?"

"We might try," said Philip, "but I fear it shall take too long to find a buyer, and then where shall we be? Without a home and without our possessions about us, that's where!"

To discover that the man she loved could be the instrument of such a predicament was a circumstance for which

Sara was unprepared. She was equally unprepared when the door opened suddenly and Hugh strode unannounced into the room.

He looked swiftly about and when his gaze fell upon Sara, it lingered there. She thought she saw a gleam of admiration in his eyes; certainly the expression on his face was the very same expression of warmth and welcome she had detected the night before at the assembly. But he made no move toward her and no soft words of affection came to his lips.

It was just as well; for if his manner was a trifle cool, it would make it, Sara thought, that much easier for her to say to him what needed to be said.

She stood and faced him with a rigid posture, her hands fixed together in a firm clasp that they may not quake and her chin raised. "I know why you have come!"

"Do you?" he asked, smiling in a manner that almost set her to trembling. "I cannot think you do, for I had planned to wait for Carville at the curb, but I discovered as I did last night, that there are some lures too strong to be denied." He paused, his eyes resting appreciatively on her face for the briefest moment before the look and his smile fell away. "What is it?" he asked, suddenly.

How like him to feign concern, she thought bitterly. How like him to squeeze every last bit of affection and trust from her! The thought of his treachery stiffened her resolve. Stubbornly, pridefully, she said, "I am aware how much money you have had from Philip and I know, too, you hold his vouchers. It is useless to deny it, for I have it on good authority that you have settled some of his debts here in town."

That was not the speech Hugh had anticipated hearing from the woman he loved. He was a little startled, as much by her tone as by her words. Though he wondered what in blue blazes might have prompted her to speak to him so, he did not betray his curiosity. He said, instead, quite mildly, "I haven't a mind to confirm or deny anything. But, pray, continue."

She squared her shoulders and drew a deep breath. "I give you my pledge that the vouchers will be redeemed. No matter what the sum, Philip's debt will be repaid. I ask only that you do not take possession of Carvington Hall."

He looked at her a moment, a slight frown between his brows, his expression a trifle puzzled. "Indeed? And just what, may I ask, convinced you it was my intent to possess Carvington Hall?"

"I had hoped you would be enough of a gentleman not to tease me!" she said, burningly aware that he had not, thus far, denied anything.

One of Hugh's dark brows shot skyward and his jaw tightened perceptively. In one stunning moment did he realize that Sara was speaking to him with perfect sincerity. He could not have been more astonished—or more furious, for to suddenly discover that the woman he loved believed him capable of extorting gaming debts from her and her brother left him in something of a confused rage.

Very well, Miss Sara Brandon-Howe! he thought. Let us see just how poor your opinion of me truly is.

It was a petty resolve, one that was unworthy of a man of his intelligence, but Hugh was suddenly seized with the notion of proving to his infuriating young love that she had grossly misjudged him.

He fixed her with a hard stare. "Oh, I shan't tease you! I was merely curious how you were able to discover my nefarious plot! Very well! You wish to repay Carville's debts! I shall take the money now, if you please."

"But—but I don't have the money," said Sara, a little stunned, "but I am very willing to make some sort of arrangement for it's repayment. I promise you shall be paid!''

"Promise? No, I thank you! In my experience, promises are made merely to be broken.''

"Not by me! I assure you, I am a woman of my word.''

"Is that so? Tell me, how much money do you have? Right now, in ready cash?''

Sara cast a frantic look at Philip, who struggled to his feet between his canes, saying, "We neither of us have any money, as well you know!''

Hugh's lip curled. "So much for promises.''

"But there must be some way to satisfy you!'' said Sara, unwilling and unable to give up. "There must be some manner in which the money may be repaid to your satisfaction.''

He watched her a moment, his expression unreadable. At last he said, with perfect calm, "There is, now that I think on it, a service I require that you might be able to provide.''

"You have only to name it!'' said Sara.

"I am in need of a housekeeper,'' he answered, with an eye to her reaction.

It was all that he hoped for. Her expression froze a moment in shock, and her hands, clasped together before her in eager anticipation, fell lifelessly away to her sides.

"A—a *housekeeper*?'' she repeated. "Is—is that all you think of me? Is that how you regard me? As nothing more than—'' She stopped, unable to trust her voice any longer.

"Yes, a housekeeper—that is your profession is it not? Come, come! I am making you a very simple proposition: I have need of someone to run my house in London. You may do so, and work off some of Carville's debt besides.''

Philip was just as stunned as his sister by such a suggestion; he raised one of his canes and shook it in Hugh's direction. "You cannot be serious! To suppose for even a moment that Sara would accept such an offer! Why, it's preposterous! She won't do it!"

"Why not?" asked Hugh, mildly. "She is merely a house-keeper, isn't she? You certainly introduced her to me as such, and I had it from Sara's own lips that there was no more relation between the two of you than that of a master and his servant. If all that you have told me is the truth, there is no reason Sara should not consider my offer." He saw the look of confusion on Philip's face. "Isn't that right, Carville?"

Young Lord Carville was laboring under a very strong emotion. For the first time since making Hugh Deverill's acquaintance, he was confronted with the consequences of his many little white lies. If he told Hugh the truth, if he told him that Sara was, in fact, his sister, he would have to face Hugh's wrath, for he didn't think a man like Devil Deverill would take kindly to the notion that he had been deceived by a country flat.

Yet he could not very well send his sister off to London with the man. Not normally perceptive, Philip had, how-ever, detected a certain attraction between Hugh and Sara. To have involved himself in their affairs would have required too much of an effort on his part so he had steered well clear of the subject. But he knew very well that he would single-handedly signal his sister's ruin if he sent her off to live in London under the same roof as Hugh Deverill. He had never before found himself in such a fix nor had he ever been caused before to see the damage he had created by living too high and too fast and leaving a string of lies in his wake. His was, however, a lesson learned too late.

Philip hobbled forward, his expression a mask of righteous anger. "Sara will never come to you in London! Never!"

"No? Not even once she hears the sum she will receive in salary?" asked Hugh, quite unruffled. He named a figure that brought a gasp from both Philip and Sara and added, "At that figure, your debts should be settled within three to four years, I should think." He allowed them both a gracious moment in which to digest this startling offer, then said, "Well? What is your answer to be, Sara?"

Philip, his face a sudden mask of red anger, shook his cane again, and said, in a choking voice, "Now—now see here, Deverill! I won't have this! I won't tolerate your treatment of my—"

"Philip!" Sara went to him and placed a calming hand upon his sleeve and said, with a very pointed look, "You musn't say anything more. Not a word, now! Mr. Deverill has made a very generous—perhaps, even outrageous— offer and I can see, truly, no reason it should not be accepted."

"Have you lost your senses?" demanded Philip, in utter astonishment. "You cannot possibly think to agree to this plan! Why, I won't have it, do you hear? I forbid you to go to London and keep house for this man! You may think me late for dinner that I never saw his true character before, but I realize now, at long last, that this man is not to be trusted!"

"I cannot see that we have any other choice," she said quietly, and after a moment she detected in his eyes a look of sad defeat. Sara turned to Hugh and set her chin again at a proud angle. "Mr. Deverill, I accept your offer. I shall go with you to London as your housekeeper for the salary you have named. I—I hope I may trust that you shall remember that ours is strictly a business relationship?"

* * *

Hugh eyed her keenly. So, she was willing to sacrifice herself for the sake of her brother, was she? Under any other circumstance he might have been impressed; in this instance, however, he would much rather she had demonstrated a bit of faith in him. As it was, he could see that she intended to stand her ground proudly but he was also aware, from the look in her eyes, that she was terribly hurt and very close to tears.

Had he been a prudent man, Hugh would have admitted to both Sara and Philip that the game had gone too far; had he been a prudent man, he would have dropped all pretense and taken Sara in his arms and assured her that he had nothing but the best and most honorable of all intentions toward her.

But then, a prudent man would never have found himself in the dubious position of discovering that the woman he loved was capable of holding him in such low esteem. That she thought him possessed of the most indecent morals was clearly evident; that it would have been a simple task to disabuse her of that notion was not a possibility he cared to entertain. He was in love with Sara and he knew very well that she was more than a little in love with him. While she had resisted her feelings for him and had even gone so far as to listen to and then believe the most scurrilous gossip concerning his character, he was largely convinced that in her heart, she cared for him. Surely by now he had proven to her that he was not as bad as Lord Westbury and his kind had painted him.

It was a matter of some importance to him that Sara realize on her own that Hugh Deverill was a man to be trusted. Even more importantly, he wanted Sara to confide at last that she was no mere housekeeper, to trust him enough to divulge the reason that had first prompted her to embark upon such a ridiculous masquerade. Clearly, she did not intend to share her secrets yet.

He said, with a slight bow, "Then it is agreed. Sara, I trust you shall have sufficient time to pack for a journey to London if I call for you at six? Good." He turned a look of bland inquiry upon Philip. "I've concluded my business here in town for today. Carville, do you wish to drive back with me to Carvington Hall?"

Philip rose up indignantly. "Certainly not! You cannot think that under the circumstances I would agree to drive three feet with you, let alone three miles!"

"So it would seem. I shall simply pack my bags, then leave. Farewell, then, Carville, and thank you for your hospitality these last weeks. Sara, I shall see you at six."

Hugh left the room just as Lord Westbury entered it. Beyond a short nod of his head, and a smile of faint triumph directed at his lordship, Hugh did not linger.

"What was *he* doing here?" asked Lord Westbury. "And why do you both look as though you have had dire news?"

It fell to Philip to tell his lordship what had just occurred. When Sara, halfway through Philip's oration, began to sob quietly, Lord Westbury rose up in righteous anger.

"I forbid it, do you hear? I utterly forbid it!" he exclaimed.

Philip shook his head, sadly. "Sara says we have no choice and she's right, dash it! We haven't!"

Lord Westbury pressed his kerchief into Sara's hand. "But you do have a choice! Sara, you do not have to go with Deverill! You know you may stay here with me for as long as you wish!"

"And allow Mr. Deverill to take Carvington Hall from us? Never! Carvington Hall is our home! It is all we have left of Papa and Mama and— Oh, don't you see? I cannot allow him to take our home from us!"

His lordship resisted an impulse to wrap a comforting arm about her shaking shoulders and said, instead, in a voice of deep confusion, "I cannot help but think you have got this wrong, somehow. I cannot think Deverill would serve you such a turn! Why after last night, I was fairly well convinced—" He stopped short, realizing that there was no point in speaking of the affection he had thought Hugh Deverill held for Sara. Instead, he remained by her side, offering what little comfort he could.

By six o'clock, Sara's tears had dried but her emotional state was no less precarious than it had been earlier. She chose to await Hugh's arrival in the drawing room, with her brother and Lord Westbury beside her. She had thought she had her emotions well in hand, but the sound of the front door chime caused her to start nervously. A moment later, when Hugh came into the room, she had to cling to her self-control by clutching her gloved hands together in a very tight grip.

Hugh entered the room and received a good portion of dagger-like stares from Philip and Lord Westbury. "Carville, Westbury! A pleasure to see you, as always," he remarked amiably, as if some social purpose had caused their paths to cross.

Lord Westbury, judging that Hugh's careless pose was beyond the pale, stepped forward and said, rather belligerently, "Deverill, I could call you out for this!"

"You could, but you won't," responded Hugh, unperturbed. His gaze swept over Philip, gone rigid with disapproval, and Sara, who, he had no doubt, had been crying. There was, too, no doubt in his mind that she was not at all looking forward to embarking upon the course he had set for her.

He ignored the prick of his conscience that told him he had been the cause of her tears and said, "It is time we were gone, I think. Are you ready, Sara?"

Chapter Eighteen

Sara looked up at Hugh, her eyes round and wide, and she said, falsely bright, "Oh, is it six so soon? I hadn't noticed. I don't suppose there is any point in prolonging the thing. Yes, let us go at once!"

"Have you made your goodbyes?"

"Yes! Yes, I have," she answered, fervently hoping that no more conversation would be required of her already trembling voice. But however much her words might quaver, she moved toward the door with admirable calm. It wasn't until she reached the doorway and Hugh met her, his hand outstretched, that she became wholly disconcerted. Almost of its own accord did her hand find its way to his waiting fingertips. His touch was warm compared to the sudden cold that seemed to seize her.

He smiled at her in a manner she was sure no employer had any right to; nor had an employer any business looking quite as handsome and elegant as he. He was dressed as always in the first stare of fashion, and he had about him the air of one who was about to embark upon nothing more strenuous than a leisurely drive along Claverton Down.

Still possessed of her hand, Hugh led Sara out into the street to his waiting carriage. Like a true gentleman, he solicitously handed her up into the vehicle; like a truly frightened young woman, she entered the carriage and sat woodenly upon the luxuriously padded seat. He joined her inside, sending her off into a short but sure moment of panic; now or never was the time for Sara to turn back; now or never was the time for her to decry having hastily accepted employment from such a man. But no sooner did she make up her mind that she had been mad to have entertained an offer to keep house for a known rogue, than she chanced to look back at Westbury house.

There, on the steps, she beheld Lord Westbury, standing beside Philip, his steadying hand on Philip's shoulder, the faces of both men filled with frowning concern. In Philip's expression she thought she detected a worry, a concern that she had not recognized there before.

Her resolve strengthened. She would not disappoint her dear brother; she would keep her end of the bargain she had struck with Hugh Deverill and would do whatever she had to do to eliminate the horrid debt Philip had accumulated.

Sara raised one gloved hand in a slight wave as the carriage lurched forward and immediately found that very hand once again claimed by Hugh Deverill. She knew a slight measure of panic on finding herself at last alone with the very man her trusted friends had warned her against, and now to find her hand enveloped within the warmth of his strong fingers quite set her nerves on edge.

She said, hoping to relieve some of the tension she felt, ''How—how long a journey is it to London, Mr. Deverill?''

''Some hours, although we won't undertake the trip today,'' he replied, with an eye to her reaction. ''We'll

make an early start of it tomorrow. Or, perhaps, the nex
day.''

Those words, so genially uttered, quite set her heart to
pounding. "To—tomorrow? But—but where, then, are w
going now? Why did you call for me *today*?"

Hugh cast her a look of mild reproach. "We have ;
bargain, you and I. You are not, I hope, planning to reneg
on your promise to me."

"Of course not! It is only—if we do not travel unti
tomorrow, I might have—Only tell me where we ar
going!''

"Still you do not trust me, eh, Sara?" he asked, quietly

"No! No, I do not!" she retorted. She snatched her hand
from his grasp and added, "I hope you shall remember tha
ours is a business relationship, and nothing more!''

"I would never presume to think more," he answered
genially.

Despite the fact that he was no longer possessed of he
hand, Sara found she could not be comfortable with Hugl
Deverill. He said nothing more to her, nor did he mak
any attempt to move close to her within the small confine
of the coach; still she remained wretchedly conscious o
him as the carriage bowled along the streets.

That he was capable of making love to her right ther
in the coach and flattering her into a submissive jelly, sh
did not doubt. While she was relieved that he had thus fa
shown no propensity for doing just so, she was equall
frightened from wondering just when such behavior migh
start. Least of all her worries was the teasing notion tha
they were not, after all, bound for London that night. Sh
had no notion where indeed she would pass that evening
but based upon Hugh Deverill's reputation, she doubte(
very much that she would find it comfortable.

Only the urgent need to save Philip and Carvington Hal
caused Sara to remain on the coach bench across fron

Hugh. She chanced a look at him and found that he was merely watching out the window, quite at his ease, as if bending housekeepers to his imperious will was an occurrence of everyday proportions to him.

The coach came to a stop and lurched a little as one of the grooms jumped down and opened the door. He made a step and Hugh alit, but he paused on the street and turned back to hold his hand out to her in a most gentlemanly fashion.

Sara hesitated, then placed her hand in his, and stepped down from the carriage. Too late did she realize that they had not yet traveled outside of the confines of Bath; too late did she realize that they were drawn up in front of one of the larger hotels in town. From the blaze of welcoming lights she could read the sign THE WHITE HART.

Before she could recover from her surprise at finding herself in such a place, Hugh was leading her up the stairs toward the front door. With every step her heart beat a little faster and when she entered the hotel and found herself in a stylish hall, enhanced by quite elegant appointments, her mouth had gone so dry as to make it impossible for her to utter a word.

Suddenly, in a flushing wave of embarrassment, all the implications of Sara's surroundings burst upon her. Never had she thought Hugh Deverill capable of such behavior. Oh, she had certainly heard all the rumors about him, and dear Lord Westbury had tried so hard to tell her, but Sara had stubbornly failed to listen to him. And now she had no one but herself to blame for finding herself in such a mortifying situation.

In the bright glow of the hall, Sara saw Hugh Deverill in a new light. Gone was the charming man who had driven her up Lansdown Hill; gone too was the graceful gentleman who had so touchingly waltzed with her in the gallery of Carvington Hall. Now, in an instant, she thought

that everything about him had changed. The faint smile
he cast her, that she had once found so handsome, now
took on a most sinister significance; and his eyes, that she
had once thought had a way of gleaming in admiration
whenever they had lit upon her, now seemed to adopt a
rather demonic glint.

He led her to the staircase and she moved quite woodenly beside him. On the second floor he gave a peremptory
knock on the first door and it opened immediately. A
stately butler bowed and ushered them into the room.
"Good evening, sir. Good evening, miss," he said, as a
footman stepped forward to accept their coats, hats, and
gloves.

Sara did not wish to give up those items so easily; she
had begun to tremble nervously and she rather suspected
that there was a good deal of goose flesh peeking out from
beneath the sleeves of the summer dress she wore, but she
was still too frightened to talk and begging to keep her
coat about her was quite out of the question.

At the far end of the room, another footman threw open
a second door. "Why don't you go into the drawing room,
Sara," suggested Hugh. "I shall join you there presently."

If he noticed that her quaking fingers had gone as cold
as ice, Hugh chose not to comment on it. Instead, he
merely lifted her hand to his lips and released her.

Knowing it was expected, but feeling as if she were walking her final steps to the gallows, Sara went into the drawing
room. She heard the door shut behind her and she whirled
about, thinking that the snap of the latch against the door
frame sounded as ominous as a jailer's key in a lock. But
when the next sound she heard was the soft voice of a
woman coming from the far side of the room, she whirled
about yet again.

The woman came forward, saying, "My dear! How
delightful to see you again! Please, won't you sit down?"

Sara recognized her immediately. Though she had seen the woman in the carriage on Lansdown Hill for only a few moments, she thought she would be able to recognize Hugh's mother anywhere.

Mrs. Deverill's presence was one of the last things Sara would have expected, and she found herself wondering, quite foolishly, if he always made it a point to have his mother attend his seductions.

"My dear," prompted Mrs. Deverill, "do you not wish to sit? I rather think you should; you're not looking at all the thing!"

She must have perceived Sara's white face, and the manner in which she was forced to clasp her hands together very tight to keep them from trembling and she seemed a little alarmed by it. She held a chair for Sara. "Please! Won't you sit here?"

Sara gratefully sank down onto the offered chair, unable to command any longer her quaking knees. "I beg your pardon, ma'am! I didn't mean to stare at you so when I came in just now, but I certainly had not expected to find you here, of all people!"

"Really? I cannot think why not. You see, this is *my* suite of rooms."

"Is it?" uttered Sara, her eyes gone wide.

"And it is my son who brought you here, you know," added Mrs. Deverill, in case there were any remaining confusion.

"Yes, I know that, but I cannot think *why* he would have done so!" she said, thinking that she was partaking of one of the oddest seductions of which she had ever heard. "You see, I thought he meant to—when I saw he had brought me to a hotel, I thought—" She stopped, knowing she had verged on a gross indiscretion.

Mrs. Deverill sat down beside her and pressed a glass of dark red wine into her hand. "Here, my dear, you must drink this. No, I insist! You look very much as though you have suffered a shock and I don't think you are in a position to make any fair judgments of your situation, right now.'

Sara obediently took a sip from her glass. The wine did nothing to ease the dryness of her throat, but it did help clear her head a little.

"There!" said Mrs. Deverill. "I see your color coming back a little. Another drink, I think and you shall be feeling quite yourself again. Yes, that's it, my dear. Now, why don' you tell me what is troubling you?"

Never, in the history of seduction, thought Sara, had a victim ever been addressed so tenderly before or welcomed so graciously by the seducer's mother. Indeed, Mrs. Deverill's expression was filled with such kind concern, Sara was not quite sure what to think. She was beginning to suspect that she had been wrong about Hugh's intentions; tha the scene of depravity and rape that had caused her to quake only moments before was, in fact, nothing more than the product of her own fertile imagination. But if he had not brought her to The White Hart for some immoral purpose, she wondered, just why *had* he brought her?

She took another fortifying sip from her glass and handed it back to Mrs. Deverill. "Thank you! I don't think I need to drink any more. At last I believe I am beginning to think quite clearly about—about, oh, so many things!'

"My child, is there anything I can do to help you in any way?" asked Mrs. Deverill, with a kindly but cautious look

Sara shook her head. "I think, though, that I should like to find Mr. Deverill. May I go in search of him?"

"You needn't search, my dear. There is a small study in the room next to this one. He took a fancy to it when he visited me earlier this week. I dare say you shall find him there."

Sara opened the door to the study. When she was inside that cozy room, she closed the door quietly behind her.

She stood there a moment, just inside the room, watching Hugh before he became aware of her presence. He was at the fireplace, staring down into the flames that danced there, a glass of dark port in one hand, and a small sheaf of papers in the other. He took a sip from his glass, then he let loose a few of the papers from his hand, and he watched them flutter down into the flames.

Sara didn't know quite what to make of such curious behavior for a man she had suspected to be capable of such hideous crimes as rape and seduction. She moved a little closer and when she was only a little behind him, she looked over his wide, strong arm and saw very clearly the writing on the papers still left in his hand.

They were gaming vouchers—Philip's gaming vouchers, she suspected, and before she could say a word, before she could utter any protest that might alter his decision, he dropped the remaining sheets into the fire.

She caught her breath and he turned about quickly.

"How long have you been standing there, Sara?"

"Long enough to see what you have done," she answered, promptly. Her eyes searched his face, seeking some expression or hint that might explain his actions. His countenance revealed nothing, however, and she was forced to ask, a little breathlessly, "Why did you burn Philip's vouchers just now?"

"Can you not guess, Sara?"

She could guess a great many things, but she didn't think her already taut nerves would suffer well another shock or embarrassment. "You have destroyed any proof that Philip owes you money. You have disposed of any reason that would compel me to go to London with you as your housekeeper."

"As my housekeeper, yes," he said, watching her reaction. "But I'm hoping you might consent to go along in another capacity."

Sara felt her heart leap into her throat. "What—wha other capacity can you mean?"

He took her hand in his and raised it as if he meant t kiss her fingers, but he paused just short of that goa Holding her hand lightly, he examined it a moment, the looked into her face. "I wonder how you could ever hav thought I would mistake such softly graceful hands for th hands of a housekeeper?"

He could not have uttered any words that could hav surprised her more. She asked, in a tone mixed of doul and wonder, "Do you mean to tell me, you *knew*? You kne all along that I was not Philip's housekeeper?"

"Not all along," he said, with a shake of his head, "bu very nearly so. I told you once, you look nothing like housekeeper. Certainly, you never behaved as one."

"Then, how *did* I behave?" she asked.

"Charmingly. Sweetly. Enchantingly."

No three words could have sounded more wonderful t Sara's ears. She asked, through a happy fog, "Even whe I said such horrid things to you?"

"Which horrid things do you mean, my love? You flun so many in my direction."

She uttered a sound that was suspiciously similar to laugh mixed with a choke. "You are horrid, horrid indeec To have let me go on so, pretending to be a servant, whe all the while you knew!"

"I knew only that I wanted to be with you, and I sti wish it. Tell me, Sara, do you think you could come to lov a rascal such as me? I know you care for me a little, but should warn you right now, caring a little will never b enough!"

"I—I don't know, exactly," she said, a little embarrassec "Is—is that how you feel about me?"

"Yes, my dear, incorrigible girl," he said, abandonin her hand for the more fulfilling prospect of holding he

his arms. "Yes, I love you and I, for one, am not too
embarrassed to admit it!"

"Than neither am I," she said, feeling quite secure in
the strength of his embrace.

"Then say it," he commanded. "Say that you love me."

"I shall, but only if you promise that I shall not be made
to supervise the servants in your London house!"

"My dear Sara," he said, tightening his hold about her,
"as my wife, of course you shall command my households,
just as easily as you command my heart."

She blushed rosily, then laying her head back against
his shoulder, she raised her face very invitingly toward his.

Hugh did the only thing a sensible man of sound constitution and healthy libido could do under such a circumstance: he kissed her quite thoroughly.

ABOUT THE AUTHOR

Nancy Lawrence lives with her family in Aurora, Colorado. She is the author of four Zebra regency romances, *Delightful Deception, A Scandalous Season, Once Upon a Christmas* and *A Noble Rogue.* Her newest Zebra regency romance, *Miss Hamilton's Hero* will be published in April 1999. Nancy loves hearing from her readers and you may write to her c/o Zebra Books. Please include a self-addressed stamped envelope if you wish a response.